LOST SECRET

LOST SECRET

The Hidden Truth of Nalanda

AKASH PASRICHA

NU VOICE
PRESS

NU VOICE
PRESS

First published by NU VOICE PRESS 2025
An imprint of Hubhawks Pvt. Ltd
www.nuvoicepress.com

ISBN: 978-81-988726-8-5

Typeset by Saanvi Graphics, Noida
Printed at Thomson Press India Ltd
Published by Nu Voice Press

"India is the cradle of the human race, the birthplace of human speech, the mother of history, the grandmother of legend, and the great-grandmother of tradition."

– Mark Twain

This barely starts to scratch the surface. A lot more needs to be understood about science, math… and industrial-scale engineering…

"We go into space. Because whatever mankind must undertake, free men must fully shape… I believe that this nation should commit itself to achieving the goal, before this decade is out, of landing a man on the moon and returning him safely to the Earth."

– John F Kennedy

And he once again proved the might of an inspired and focused people…

This book is dedicated to us, to society, and to the promise of a better tomorrow

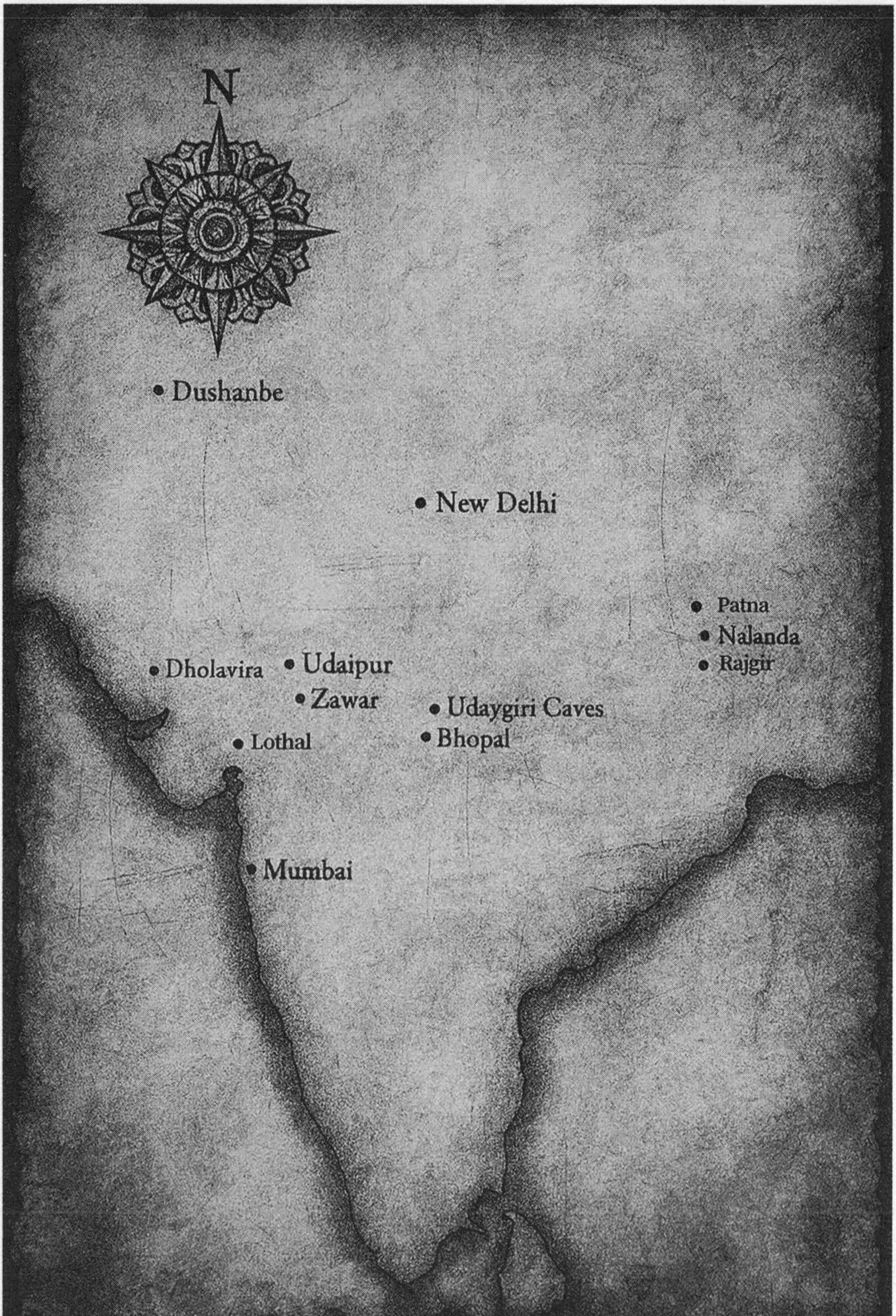

Figure 1: *Map of Major Harappan (Indus Valley) and Early Historic Sites in the Indian Subcontinent*

Table of Contents

1
Rajgir

Day 1 | 0300 hrs

A CELL PHONE IN A ROBUST LEATHER COVER, DIRTY AND WORN by rough handling, suddenly came to life and started buzzing insistently on the nightstand. Superintendent of Police Kabir opened his eyes just enough to stare at it irritably. He had been promised that there would be no more midnight emergency calls at this new post in the small town of Rajgir. And certainly, none from the chief minister of the state.

What could have possibly happened in this small village that would lead to a call on his phone from the chief minister at this unearthly hour? Still in his boxers, Kabir answered the phone as he got up and walked towards the moonlit window overlooking the serene surroundings. He instinctively glanced towards the bed where Vani would have been fast asleep, only to find the emptiness that mirrored his heart. They had dreamed of being in an oasis of tranquillity, and Rajgir would have been perfect for them.

"How can I help you, Minister *ji*?" said Kabir, now awake and alert. He always added the '*ji*' when speaking with ministers and other important people. It seemed appropriate.

"Kabir, there has been an incident near you. I am sending you the location. I am on my way as we speak. I need you to get there right away. More when I see you in a few minutes," he said and hung up. Kabir's phone pinged with the location.

A few minutes? Kabir thought to himself. *The chief minister must already be in town if he is reaching in a few minutes. Why was I not informed of his visit?*

In a fast and deliberate motion, he reached for his jeans, carelessly thrown on the armchair. The streaming moonlight accentuated every muscle on his arched back as he slipped the tight denim on his muscular legs. He reckoned that a t-shirt and the standard khaki police jacket would be fine at this hour. Kabir tied the laces of his leather boots firmly. He preferred them snug as they gave him a better grip on the pedals while riding. Rather than being cooped up in the police Jeep, he liked to feel the wind in his hair as he cut through the heavy, humid monsoon air riding his Royal Enfield motorcycle.

He was one of the few who were hand-picked and brought in during the formative years of the National Investigation Agency, an elite counter terrorism force. His successes on challenging and sensitive missions had gained him the trust of the organisation and put him on a fast track to leadership. Until tragedy struck and almost broke him. His body and mind had been coming apart at the seams when he moved to Rajgir. Being in this town had allowed him time to slow down and heal.

It only took him a few minutes to reach the location sent by the chief minister. Instinctively, Kabir looked around and assessed the scene he had been summoned to.

A wrought iron gate that was rather large for the narrow pathway that followed was half open. The faded indigo-washed bungalow surrounded by dried-up, dead brush was dimly lit by the moonlight.

As his motorcycle reached the gate, a well-built man in khaki fatigues approached him. He was comfortably in control of a sub-machine gun, making it feel safe rather than threatening.

Kabir saw the silhouette of a dead body, likely the guard of the estate, lying to the side of the gate. A quick glance showed that the dead body was not that of an ordinary watchman, but of someone who had spent a lifetime preparing for combat. Kabir was well-built, muscular and had a distinguished look about him, but this guard looked like he had almost sculpted his body with utmost care and precision.

The clean bullet hole on the forehead had clearly come from afar—too far for his eyes to have seen it coming. It was surely the job of a professional sniper, made easy by the acres of foliage and the failing lights on the estate.

"They are expecting you inside." The commando guarding the gate seemed to know who he was. He gestured towards the verandah at the entrance of the bungalow. In sharp contrast to the drying lawn, the verandah was brimming with lush green plants and blooming flowers.

Kabir nodded as his eyes scanned the surroundings. All that he had seen so far made him certain that this was not a crime scene that fit the serene outskirts of Rajgir.

With an added sense of urgency, Kabir climbed the brick steps that led to a polished, dark teak door. The heaviness and antiquity of the door became apparent to him as he pushed it open to the sound of creaking hinges.

The entrance hall was a spacious chamber with a high ceiling. It housed what looked like valuable artefacts that were displayed in glass cases, giving it the feel of a museum or an antique shop, straight out of a 1920s French movie.

Prominently placed on the front wall was a large, well-lit display protected with a thick glass, of two circular tablets that looked like they were made of unburnt clay.[1] The tablets were inscribed with a script that Kabir did not recognise. The label on the display placed the tablets in the second–first century BCE. There were other artefacts around the display that were most likely from the same era.

A beautifully crafted and well-preserved terracotta bird with extended wings sat on one side. On the other was a black on-red pottery sherd decorated with a fish-scale pattern. The inscription placed it in Kalibanga, circa 2000-1750 BCE.[2]

To his left was another room, which had a lower ceiling than the entrance hall. Two men stood there looking towards Kabir. They'd heard the door creak open. A body lay slumped against the wall near them.

"Come, Kabir, this way. Glad you could get here quickly. I hope you did not tell anyone else?" asked the gentleman with greying hair and a well-groomed beard.

The chief minister, Tiwari *ji*, as he was popularly known, was wearing a casual *kurta* over a pair of fashionable jeans. He seemed to fit right into the stereotype of the new breed of politicians. Seemingly, satisfied with the material world, the young-at-heart decision-makers saw their work as a service to the population that had elected them. His tone was friendly, but had just enough authority to get Kabir's attention.

"Tiwari *ji*," Kabir acknowledged him with a slight bow, so as to dispense with more formal spoken greetings.

Kabir was surprised to find that he recognised the second man too. Mr V. Nair was the deputy chief of the National Investigation Agency and in charge of field operations for covert assignments. He was also Vani's father. Unlike Kabir, Nair was formally dressed and seemed to have more grey hair than Kabir remembered. It was Nair who had suggested that Kabir move to Rajgir after Vani's death.

Kabir's instinctive ability to suppress the rising tide of emotions and to focus on the moment came in handy. However, the utter surprise of seeing Nair at the scene forced the obvious in Kabir's mind as they shook hands. *Why are you here?*

"Kabir, I know there must be a lot of questions on your mind right now," Tiwari spoke in a reassuring tone, sensing the circuits firing in Kabir's brain. "For now, let's focus on finding out why Professor Ghosh asked Nair and me here tonight. Perhaps more important than finding the killers is to determine what they learned before they killed him."

With his balding head dropping to the right and mouth slightly open, the professor looked like he was deep in slumber rather than dead. Kabir observed the slight blue tone of the skin of the otherwise uninjured dead body. *Asphyxiation*, he thought to himself.

Nair was a polite and soft-spoken man who seemed to measure his words as he spoke in a drawl. He was also known to anticipate and plan for events not foreseen by others. Kabir wondered—*was I posted in Rajgir because Nair knew something like this could happen?*

"Dr Subhajit Ghosh was a renowned professor of archaeology who had received several accolades, including the presidential honour. He was a key member and the shepherd of the team that was conducting the excavation at Giriyak, one of the Nalanda University sites nearby. He had been associated with the ASI (Archaeological Survey of India) for many years, having started his career with a hands-on excavation of Nalanda University. He was very well-liked and respected by his students and the faculty. Everyone affectionately called him 'Professor *ji*'," Nair told Kabir.

"Dr Ghosh, Nair, and I were inseparable in boarding school. Even after we graduated, we kept in touch. Our lives did not cross paths much, but we were still close," Chief Minister Tiwari added.

"Kabir, there is a lot more at stake here than what appears at first glance," said Nair. "I'm sure you must have figured that out by now," he added in acknowledgement of Kabir being a gifted Intelligence officer. "Professor Ghosh was an exceptional archaeologist. He had discovered a few artefacts of unusual significance during the excavations at Giriyak," said Nair, his face wearing an intense expression. "We don't know exactly how, but we believe that some powerful international players also became aware of these relics and seem to be ready to kill for them. We need to recover what was taken and neutralise the threat."

"How will we know what was taken?" Kabir asked the

obvious question. "And why do we need to find what was taken before we chase the killers?"

"You may have a point," conceded Nair. "We did not want the forensic teams coming here to look for clues and disturb the crime scene before we could figure out what was missing. But please feel free to look around while we wait for Reeya."

"Who is Reeya?" asked Kabir, just as they heard the sounds of a car outside, and of twigs and branches being crushed.

"Well, she is here, so we can get on with the introductions directly," Nair said and turned towards the door.

A slim, female figure could be seen climbing the steps, two at a time, swiftly approaching them. She moved as if she knew her way around the bungalow and came to stand before the group. Her wavy, dishevelled hair and still sleepy eyes behind her glasses were clear indications that she had just jumped out of bed and hurried to reach the scene. The black *churidar* tights and rust-coloured *kurta* showed she valued comfort and yet could confidently carry mainstream fashion. The nerdy look seemed just a disguise.

She let out a small gasp at the sight of the body and kneeled over the professor, stopping short of touching him. With both hands covering her face, she allowed herself a moment to grieve. Though visibly disturbed by what she saw, she did not seem shocked. It seemed almost as if she expected what lay before her. She looked keenly at the professor's lifeless body, as though scanning for clues.

Reeya heaved a deep sigh and steadied herself as she stood facing the three men who were respectfully giving her the space to compose herself. The quiver of her chin betrayed the brave effort to hold back her tears, yet instinctively, she wiped her eyes.

"They took his bracelet. I don't know how they knew of its relevance, but he had suspected that they might," she said to the three men who looked at her expectantly for further explanation.

"My apologies. I will explain," said Reeya as she paused to gather her thoughts and turned towards the chief minister to address him. "Thank you for informing me, Tiwari *ji*. I got here as soon as I got your call."

"I am assuming you both are from the intelligence agency." She looked at Kabir and then Nair as she spoke. "Professor *ji* had briefed me about you and said to trust no one other than the three of you."

Without waiting for acknowledgements, she continued, "Later, I will explain what I know in detail. For now, we must look for what Professor *ji* needed us to find. He would have left enough information to guide us."

The room was filled with antiquities. Reeya's eyes moved across the room, expertly scanning every object that adorned the space. She paused to look closely at a few while continuing her monologue.

"Professor *ji* had been sent a copy of a manuscript fragment that indicated the knowledge of an artefact that could change the course of the future. He could not decipher the full picture of what was being described. I know it sounds improbable, but he mentioned nuclear fission," Reeya said absent-mindedly.

The three men exchanged glances as she mentioned nuclear fission in a matter-of-fact tone. It was apparent that they were all equally clueless about what she was saying.

Her eyes were on a fragment of a body armour from the ninth century CE.[3] It appeared to have been made by weaving chains of a metal alloy.

"We have all heard of Nalanda, which rose as a university undoubtedly by the year 450 CE and continued to function robustly until at least the 12th century, becoming the longest running centre for higher learning,"[4] Reeya said, reciting mechanically what she had read in the history books. "I am working to ascertain claims that it was already functioning by around the third century BCE. In all the years of it being a repository of knowledge for the known universe, it has held many secrets.

"Professor *ji* was an authority on all things Nalanda and was recognised as such nationally and internationally. But for some reason, the manuscript copy he received spooked him. It could be due to the mention of something like nuclear fission, but I sensed he felt threatened as well." She paused and looked towards the chief minister, "That's when he called you."

Her eyes were busy scanning the room as she spoke, this time stopping at a sixth-century CE terracotta tablet inscribed in Brahmi script.[5]

"I think, after your discussion with him, he was even more on edge, and he became very secretive. I don't know what you two discussed," she turned to the chief minister, half-expecting him to reveal his conversation with the professor. "But Professor *ji* warned me not to trust anyone, soon thereafter."

As her gaze wandered over the paintings that hung around the room, it was suddenly arrested by a miniature painting depicting a hunting scene—an emperor riding a horse in pursuit of prey.

To the untrained eye, it blended harmoniously with all the other paintings hanging on the walls of the room. But Reeya looked at it quizzically and softly mumbled, "What's a 16th-century Mughal painting doing here? The rest of the paintings all belong to a far older period."

She reached out to remove it from the wall and placed it upside down on the table. Expertly dislodging the painting from its frame, she laid it face down.

Reeya recognised the professor's handwriting on a note stuck on the back of the canvas:

The local furnace did not make the metal, but it is keeping it safe.
The path from the last cave, where the oldest iron pillar was erected, will complete the Giriyak half of the tablet.

There was a pin-drop silence in the room. The three men looked up expectantly from the note at Reeya's bowed head, waiting for her to make sense of the cryptic clue.

2

Desert *Bazaar*

A few months ago…

WITH A LOUD BUZZER, THE RED LIGHT TURNED GREEN ON THE console over the doorway leading out of the belly of a C-17. It was a large transport carrier that was flying over the rugged terrain along the Afghan-Tajik border. The C-17 carefully deviated just enough from its sanctioned flight path.

The expert high-altitude paratroopers, now fully protected by thick, black, skintight fabric, made some last-minute adjustments to their gear as they secured their oxygen masks. The four men were well trained for the mission they were embarking on. They were going to intercept an exchange of a lethal next-generation nerve gas that was going to be taking place in the desert *bazaar*.

The desert *bazaar* was a high-stakes marketplace where global underworld arms dealers traded with terrorist organisations. The vast and rugged terrain made it inhospitable for any law enforcement agencies trying to maintain control of the area, and at the same time, made it easy for those who were one with the terrain—the small, nameless terrorist groups.

They could move about fluidly and disappear in the labyrinth of mountain caves and underground bunkers.

The loud alarm in the plane announced that it was time for action. The large cargo door in the underbelly of the C-17 opened, allowing the paratroopers to jump off and one by one disappear in the darkness. Nair wished Kabir luck as he prepared to follow his men into the darkness.

Kabir looked at the deputy chief and saw the warmth in his eyes. He had wondered how Mr Nair would react when he found out that his daughter, Vani, and Kabir were very serious about each other and had taken their relationship to the next level by choosing to live together. She had confided in her parents just a few days ago.

He had not had the chance to discuss the matter with Mr Nair, and they both knew that this was not the time, or the place, to have a personal conversation. The warmth and respect that were in each man's eyes would have to suffice for now.

The deputy chief was still digesting the news of his daughter being involved with Kabir in what seemed like a joyous relationship. Without a doubt, he loved his daughter more than anything and anyone else in the world. He had always supported Vani in whatever she did—studies, career, or boyfriends—he had never imposed his decisions or lifestyle on her and had always wanted her to become the strong, independent woman she was today.

Like every father, he was also very protective of her and wanted to make sure that his little girl had chosen the right partner for herself. He was looking forward to meeting

Kabir and Vani together, to know more about their plans for the future.

The deputy chief snapped back to the present and stared into the empty space as Kabir was swallowed into the darkness behind his team. The ruckus made by the wind and engine subsided as the cargo door closed behind them.

"Best of luck," Nair whispered softly into the empty space.

Piercing the cold of the night, four men parachuted to the designated location, landing within a few metres of each other. Each man automatically disengaged from his chute and stowed any equipment no longer needed.

The area was as familiar to them as studying it closely on a map could make it. Spotting the landmarks they had committed to memory, the team quickly reached the designated meeting spot. As planned, Abdul, their local guide, was waiting for them, ready to take them to the *bazaar*.

Abdul was an expert in the terrain as he had lived in the area since he was a teenager. With a greying beard and bushy eyebrows, he was now an ardent advocate of peace and normalcy for his region. He had home-schooled his children, keeping them shielded from the rhetoric of violence, and hoped for a more productive life for them.

"Good to see you, Abdul," Kabir greeted him, as both men embraced firmly, despite Abdul's large belly coming in the way. "You are being well fed, my friend," Kabir said with a laugh.

"Good to see you too. It has been a while," Abdul replied, smilingly. The two had worked together before and had mutual respect for each other's ability and integrity.

"We are on a tight schedule." Pointing to his modified four-wheel drive Land Rover that was well-suited to the terrain, Abdul instructed, "Get in, everyone. Most delegates to the *bazaar* are already there."

"How is the family?" Kabir inquired as everyone settled down in the spacious vehicle.

Abdul had been looking forward to meeting Kabir as he felt he could talk freely to him. As they drove to the bazaar, he filled Kabir in on the latest about his daughter.

"She is now a teenager and wants a smartphone. I don't even know how they get to know about these gadgets. We don't even have cell coverage in this area!" Abdul laughed. "But trust a teenage girl to know what she wants."

He was a good father, and although he wished for a better life for his children, he had some rather rigid notions of what was good for them. Like many who had grown up in humble homes, he was resistant to providing his kids with luxuries. Unlike the rest of the world, to him, a mobile phone was not a necessity.

As they approached the *bazaar*, Kabir gestured to his men to jump out of the moving vehicle as it slowed down on the sharp curves. Stopping the car could have drawn unwanted attention. The snipers hurried to take up vantage positions.

Kabir's life had been full of such high-risk missions. Working for the National Investigation Agency had meant active involvement in high-profile and high-stakes counterintelligence. The newly formed agency had already earned a reputation for preventing catastrophic attacks.

Even though he was one of the youngest recruits, Kabir had proved his worth and earned the trust of his seniors on several occasions. Mr Nair, the deputy chief, appreciated the candour, passion, and skill that Kabir brought to the table.

Abdul continued down the winding road towards the *bazaar*. The tall, rugged peaks on either side of the narrow road looked ominous in the moonlight. At a distance, Kabir could see the shimmer of fast-flowing water. He could also spot lights coming from a cluster of tents, faint yet discernible. Kabir was glad that his sniper team consisted of world-class marksmen. For anyone less skilled, it would be a difficult shot from that distance.

Abdul and Kabir approached a makeshift barrier, which was guarded by three men. They were carrying machine guns and other armaments strapped over their traditional woollen *perahan tunban* that shielded them from the cold in the harsh evenings.

Abdul stopped the vehicle and exchanged pleasantries with one of the guards, as the other two inspected the vehicle with their torchlights. Satisfied, they allowed the occupants to pass on to a narrow, cobbled-stone road that cut through a grassy patch.

Kabir studied the terrain carefully to see if there were any areas that offered a safe passage out in case of a hasty retreat. There were none. He knew he'd have to rely on the snipers perched on the rocky cliffs above.

A short drive led them to a makeshift parking lot outside a tent large enough to house a supermarket. The main tent and the several smaller tents surrounding it were made of an opaque fabric that did not allow light to escape. *It was an added precaution to prevent surveillance or drone attacks*, Kabir inferred.

There was just enough light in the grounds to illuminate any suspicious movements. The compound was swarming with guards who looked ready to shoot anyone who did not seem to belong. There would be no questions asked and no justifications given.

There was a stark change of scene inside the tent. The place was warm and well-lit with a stage in the middle. A belly dancer was performing to live music as those passing by ogled her curves.

There were hundreds of stalls, neatly organised into rows, each displaying and selling wares, quite like any other market. Droves of people moved around as they enquired, examined, or negotiated for the deadly wares that were up for sale. The whole setup was an amalgamation of a street market and a business convention.

Entering the tent, they veered right along some unoccupied stalls. Kabir first wanted to establish a contingency plan. After a short distance, they slid into an opening that led to the service area and doubled back along the periphery. Kabir knew there was no danger of their actions being caught on surveillance cameras, as these were strictly prohibited in a *bazaar* where buyers wanted their identities shielded. They installed several small, remote-controlled explosive devices they were carrying near the entrance. The tents were designed to withstand such explosions, but they would still serve as a cover or distraction, if needed.

Having placed the explosives, they walked back through the service area and into a narrow aisle, mingling with the crowd. Following their instructions, they moved towards the western side of the market, where there were fewer people and larger stalls.

Kabir stayed focused on finding the stall that had been indicated in their intelligence briefing. Painstaking background work had gone into providing Kabir and his contact the cover that had allowed them to get this far. Now it was up to them.

They approached a stall that was not carrying any visible merchandise. Kabir confirmed that it was the stall they were looking for by checking that the small numbers posted on a plastic signboard over the stall matched what he had been given. The large, distinguished-looking Caucasian man in a tailored suit, seated a tad awkwardly on the *diwan* placed towards the front of the stall, was engrossed in his laptop.

A guard in a t-shirt accentuating his large biceps sat towards the back of the stall, fidgeting with a touchpad device, seemingly oblivious to the *bazaar* around him. A chain bound his wrist to a steel briefcase.

If the intelligence report was correct, the glass tubes containing a deadly virus would be encased within a titanium cylinder in that steel briefcase. This next-generation fast-acting virus could quickly annihilate a large section of a densely populated city.

Kabir's biggest concern was the state-of-the-art security the briefcase came with. It was supposed to be armed to explode and release enough toxic nerve gas to kill anyone in its proximity if tampered with.

Walking casually, Kabir entered the stall with Abdul just a step behind him. He proceeded to place a metallic card on the table next to the man's laptop. The card was embossed with a series of small, seemingly random squares and lines, forming a code.

The suited man looked up from his laptop and gestured for Kabir and Abdul to sit on the *diwan* next to him. He proceeded to bring out his smartphone and scan the metal card. A green light and a *beep* made Kabir relax as he knew their cover had worked.

"The credentials check out. The terms of agreement stand as discussed previously. I will need the payment here and now. Will it be cash or credit?" joked the man, knowing very well that the briefcase Abdul was carrying already answered his question. His slight accent betrayed his Eastern European origins. "Bring it in."

Kabir looked meaningfully at the rolled-up curtains at the entrance of the stall, indicating that he'd like privacy. As the man got up to close the curtains, Kabir stood up, appearing to place his briefcase on the *diwan* as if to allow for inspection of the currency in it. But just as the curtains were rolled down, Kabir sprang to action. In one smooth motion, he removed his silenced handgun from its holster under his jacket and shot both men in the head, killing them instantly.

Abdul peeped outside the curtains to ensure no one had heard them. Kabir secured his gun as Abdul quickly moved to open the briefcase placed on the *diwan* to reveal a stack of bearer bonds. It was the currency of choice in the black market. Moving the bearer bonds to the side, he proceeded to dislodge a thin metallic canister and, in a choreographed move, handed it to Kabir.

Kabir sprayed the contents of the canister on and around the lock of the steel briefcase that was still chained to the wrist of the dead man. The liquid refrigerant in the cannister instantly froze the lock and the electronics behind it, disabling the triggering mechanism, which allowed Kabir to pry the lock open to reveal a titanium cylinder secured in a foam cut-out matching the description of what he was looking for.

He immediately removed the cylinder from the casing and carefully placed it in a cushioned compartment in his own briefcase. Both men then quickly walked out of the stall.

The steel briefcase, chained to the dead man's wrist, still had a small explosive that would go off once the triggering mechanism thawed. It would also release the deadly nerve toxin that would kill anyone in the immediate proximity of the stall. Kabir and Abdul anticipated that it would take a few minutes for that to happen, and they wanted to be well clear of the tent before the explosion.

The two men walked at a casual, yet deliberate pace, being careful not to draw attention to themselves. The market was full of paranoid buyers and sellers. And even though each entrant had been vetted carefully, most of those present were well armed and trigger-happy.

Abdul exchanged a casual farewell with the guard at the doorway as they cleared out of the tent. They proceeded to the Land Rover under the watchful eyes of the guards who surrounded the place.

Kabir tightly held on to the remote detonator of the explosive devices they'd placed at the periphery of the tent in his hand, his thumb ready to press the switch. He was hoping that he would not need to use the distraction offered by them, but he also knew that the frozen triggering mechanism of the briefcase could thaw at any moment. And as they started to drive, they heard its muffled explosion.

3

Dushanbe

ALARMED, A FLURRY OF GUARDS STARTED SCREAMING ORDERS at the duo to stop. As they continued to drive, the guards opened fire at the Land Rover. Kabir pressed the trigger, and the devices at the edges of the tent exploded. The explosion took down the first line of guards that were shooting at them, buying them a precious few seconds before the next line took their place.

Abdul drove as fast as possible on the narrow road towards the exit barrier. Two small, but highly manoeuvrable, open jeeps appeared in the open field, firing as they chased after the Land Rover.

It was time for the snipers to do their job. Perched high above the action, but watching it carefully, a sniper carefully aimed at the driver of the first jeep and pressed the trigger. The bullet made a clean hole in the windshield and hit the driver. The vehicle lost control and slid sideways, tumbling as it fell off the elevated road.

The guards at the barrier, having seen the commotion, had started shooting at the approaching Land Rover, cueing the next sniper to take aim and clear the way for Kabir and Abdul. One by one, the snipers took down the threats that stood in the duo's path.

Abdul crashed through the barrier and continued to drive as best as he could while dodging bullets. More vehicles joined the chase, but Kabir heard the echo of metal crashing into the hilly terrain as the snipers eliminated the threats.

The gunfight lasted only a few minutes, though it felt like an eternity to Abdul. He drove on the designated route while the snipers continued to hold back anyone who tried to follow. As Abdul approached, they ran down the hill to jump into the Land Rover, continuing to shoot at any approaching vehicle through the open windows, as they headed for safety.

A long but uneventful drive got Kabir and the team to Dushanbe in Tajikistan. It had been a sleepy town until recently, but was now hurriedly modernising itself. In addition to its rich history deriving from its location on the ancient Silk Route, Dushanbe now also offered amenities and experiences that modern tourists could enjoy.

The safe house was a small, nondescript house attached to a repair shop on the outskirts of the city. As he pulled into the shop, Abdul laughed at the irony as his car did need some repairs after the adventurous chase.

Kabir met with the owner, and they exchanged a few words to establish identities. Kabir would normally have felt relieved, handing over the ominous titanium cylinder. Today, somehow, preventing an imminent massacre was not helping put his anxiety at ease.

Normally, a drive after a successful mission would have meant catching up on sleep. But the knowledge that he would be meeting Mr Nair for dinner kept him awake. He could foresee that the meeting would not be business as usual. His relationship with Vani would come up, and he was aware that Mr Nair might not be happy about their having moved in together.

His mind, trained to explore all possible outcomes of an encounter, did exactly that as he got into a nondescript car that would take him to the hotel for the needed rest before the team was debriefed the next day. None seemed like an easy course of action, making him nervous about the dinner tonight. He tried to direct his thoughts towards the hot shower he was craving as he went through the mechanical process of checking in at the hotel.

Kabir was not expecting to see Vani at the hotel. His heart skipped a beat when he noticed her sitting comfortably, sipping a colourful summery cocktail. The fiery rose colour matched her dress, which accentuated her gorgeous curves.

Kabir was instantly reminded of the first time he had seen her at the officers' ball right after he was commissioned. The satin black hair over her shoulders seemed even silkier than when he remembered first touching it, three years ago. He smiled to himself and hoped that he'd always feel this way about her.

He felt his exhaustion and anxiety evaporate just looking at her. She always had that effect on him. The dinner with Mr

Nair no longer seemed daunting, knowing she would be by his side. He could sense her watchful eye on him as he traced his way to her. She walked over to greet him with an embrace and a kiss.

"What are you doing here?" was all that Kabir could say as he pulled himself away. "Your dad will kill me if he sees us together like this."

Vani smiled understandingly at the reaction. She was amused that despite being one of the toughest agents in the field, Kabir was scared of his girlfriend's father.

"Stop being so scared of him! He won't say a thing to you. I'll be joining you for dinner tonight and promise to protect you from him," she mocked, as they headed to his room.

The magical ring in Vani's laugh as she teased Kabir always touched a chord in his heart. He followed her as she took the key card from his hands. They got into the elevator as she punched the floor on the lift panel, holding hands. Her thumb stroked the back of his hand as he lifted his to caress her cheek. They looked at each other with the longing of two souls who had been kept apart far too long.

They let themselves in, and as soon as the door closed behind them, Vani put her arms around his neck and reached for his mouth with her lips. It was slow and deliberate, and Kabir felt the heat he knew only one way of dissipating. He lifted her up as she wrapped her legs around him and carried her to the bed.

They had the whole afternoon together. And both were thankful and determined to make the most of it. Only the room service, which would come later to tidy the room, would know just how thankful.

As the afternoon gave way to dinner time, Kabir and Vani made their way through the crowded restaurant, walking towards the table where the Deputy Chief was sitting. They couldn't help but notice his eyes following them as they approached. It only added to the nervousness Kabir was having a hard time hiding.

Vani walked up to her dad and gave him a tight, affectionate hug as he rose to take his daughter in his arms. Kabir stood there awkwardly, trying to think of something clever to say that would impress his girlfriend's father. Taking the safer course, he just nodded as he went for a firm handshake.

Sensing Kabir's nervousness, Nair decided to help him out. "Good work today, Kabir. You may have saved several thousand lives," he said, carefully avoiding the specifics, as they sat down.

Kabir could not think of anything to say other than a nervous "Thank you, sir."

Nair patiently sipped on his wine, catching up with his daughter while Kabir flipped through the menu hurriedly, trying to find something to order. Vani kicked him under the table, gesturing with her eyes that he should talk to her father.

Kabir reminded himself that he had been in worse situations and handled them far better than he was doing now. But before he could speak, a waiter approached the table. Vani could see the relief that Kabir felt at having been saved by the bell and smiled. Everyone placed their order.

Finally, Vani said, "Dad, Kabir and I wanted to talk to you about our relationship. You and Mom know that we've been seeing each other for a while now." She paused and looked towards Kabir.

It took Kabir all his courage to come up with the next words, "We wanted to have a ceremony to get your blessings as we feel it is time for us to be together."

Dinner went surprisingly well after that. Nair was absolutely delighted that Kabir and Vani wanted to take their relationship to the next level. The three of them had a good time as they enjoyed the delicious food, sharing some good laughs and discussing their future aspirations, both personal and professional.

Vani was extremely glad to see two of the most important men in her life bonding. And Nair couldn't be prouder of his daughter finding the perfect gentleman as her partner.

It would be a memory that Kabir would revisit many times in the future. Vani was clear that they should have only the most basic ceremonies for their wedding, donating the money saved to charity. Kabir realised once again how much he admired Vani for the unambiguity of her beliefs and her courage in expressing them.

Kabir caught himself thinking that if it were possible to love her more than he already did, he would. But for now, they both had to make up for the time they had spent apart. And a life-altering decision was not about to stand in their way.

Dinner was just a short break for Kabir and Vani as they picked up where they had left off. They made love through the night and into the morning hours, aware that they would soon be separated again to pursue their professional lives.

Having spent an invigoratingly exhausting night, they packed and headed to the car Vani had rented the day before. Kabir settled the bills and tipped the staff, while Vani continued to load the luggage in the car.

She was used to travelling light and effortlessly fit their luggage in the trunk of the car. He marvelled at her ability to navigate the world with the same ease that she showed packing her luggage in the car. Kabir had always liked her independence and confidence. It was one more reason for him to admire her.

Vani glanced towards Kabir as she moved towards the driver's seat, to see if he was done with the check-out. He smiled as he waved at her through the glass wall that separated the curb-side parking from the hotel lobby.

The explosion that followed crumbled the entire life that Kabir had built around the hope of being with Vani forever. As if in slow motion, he saw the bright flash emanate from the car that Vani was waiting in. He could see the fragments of the car being propelled in all directions as the flash became larger and shattered the glass of the hotel lobby. He heard the deafening sound of the explosion and was thrown backwards, along with everyone else standing nearby.

In a daze, and with his ears still ringing from the explosion, he managed to get up and look towards where Vani had been.

His mind was determined to run towards her, with his heart hammering with desperate hope. Every part of the body clung to the hope that Vani was behind the blur that the world was turning into. But the legs betrayed him as he collapsed into the chaos.

"Vani!" he shouted in excruciating pain as he bled and broke inside. It would be a shout that would wake him up every time he managed to sleep, for the foreseeable future.

That explosion was meant for me. His mind started to consume all that was left of him, in survivor's guilt.

4
Ajatshatru Stupa

KABIR DID NOT KNOW WHY NAIR HAD PICKED RAJGIR FOR HIM to recuperate. What he did know was that he'd be useless until he was less broken. To feel alive again, he needed Vani or at least avenge her death.

Kabir respected Nair and could see him hurting just as much at losing Vani. But he trusted the man as his deputy chief. The old man would know what was best.

"Kabir, take some time off from these high-profile assignments. Go to Rajgir. I'll set something up for you there. Maybe a stint in the local police. Go, take a break." Mr Nair had said, betraying his emotions. "Vani will not come back, but I don't want to lose a good agent—or a friend. At least there will not be any midnight calls to wake you up and put you on a plane to somewhere."

Kabir was thankful for the advice. He had managed to find some peace in this new town. His days were spent helping with the simple needs of the farmers and cattle herders. His excruciating pain was slowly ebbing and giving way to imagining Vani in everyday settings like negotiating with streetside vegetable vendors. It was becoming easier to feel the relief in his heart. The small town did not have much crime and allowed him plenty of free time. But he needed to keep engaged to stay afloat. Fixing a plough here, a pulley there and sometimes helping the children with their homework assignment, made him feel like his life wasn't wasting away. He had also helped in the birth of a baby in the field as the mother had gone into labour. It was exhilarating and somehow healing to help bring a life into this world.

Kabir had managed to find time to explore the quaint village. Being a physically active person, one of his favourite activities was to jog on the 48-km wall that was built to encircle Rajgir prior to the sixth century BCE. The wall, averaging 5.2m in thickness, was breathtakingly massive.[6] It somehow reminded him of a section of the Great Wall of China that he had once visited. Mid-stride, he pictured Vani at his side, her bright smile daring him to quicken his pace and catch up. A sharp pang gripped his chest, but he drove his legs onward, finding that the burn in his muscles helped silence the ache in his heart.

Kabir was intrigued by the town's historical past and its many mysteries. His colleagues would tell him the ancient history, though Kabir wasn't sure what to believe. They proudly informed him of the transformation of Rajgir from a political centre to a religious centre during the sixth and fifth centuries BCE, when Buddha and Mahavira flourished and spent considerable time there.[7]

Did the wall exist back then? Had Buddha and Mahavira walked this path?, he wondered.

He was not a voracious reader, but had read up a little bit on Rajgir. It was an archaeological site, dating back to prehistoric times.[8] It was also known by the names of Girivraja and Rajagriha[9]. It served as the capital of the Magadha Empire before 500 BCE.[10] Excavations done in the 1950s have established a culture that used Northern Black Polish Ware (NBPW) dating to the fifth century BCE or earlier.[11] The discoveries over a scattered region indicated a thriving civilisation over a substantial geographic swath.

Present day

Day 1 | 0430 hrs

As the four stood near the professor's lifeless body, Nair felt it was time to share the background information he knew. "We had been tipped off that a crime syndicate had come into possession of an ancient manuscript. Our informant believed that it was of Greek origin, and described extreme heat, possibly due to a nuclear reaction." Kabir and Reeya stared at him as they digested the words. "There is always fake information floating around about ancient nuclear devices, so we did not pay much heed to this. In fact, Tiwari *ji* and I had lunch together and joked about discussing it with Dr Ghosh.

"When Dr Ghosh called to inform me of the manuscript, I was alarmed. I wasn't particularly bothered about the nuclear fission bit, but the fact that a crime syndicate may be in possession of an ancient manuscript did give me some sleepless nights. I may have alarmed Dr Ghosh as I mentioned that to him. In retrospect, rightly so," Chief Minister Tiwari added.

"I became concerned when Tiwari *ji* informed me about his conversation with Dr Ghosh. We tried identifying the syndicate, but none of the leads panned out," Nair continued. "Now that I know he had linked that heat generation to a nuclear fission reaction, I regret not providing him more security," Nair lamented. "I knew he'd solve it. But I had not expected the killers to be this ruthless or sophisticated. Just posting one commando was obviously not enough."

Chief Minister Tiwari broke the silence as everyone absorbed what Nair had said. "Reeya, do you know what the professor wanted us to find?"

"No, I don't know what the discovery was that shook Professor *ji*. But whatever it was, I'm sure it is significant and unique. A few days back, he did indicate to me that he was close to piecing the puzzle together. And it seems he found the missing link," Reeya continued, making an obvious effort to keep her voice steady.

She felt a sense of loss rising from deep within her stomach. She sat down on the couch in the room and looked around at all the relics to which the professor had dedicated his life. She relived the moments of kindness she experienced when she had first visited the professor's house. He had been patient and kind as he indulged Reeya by sharing stories about each artefact she had been curious about. A tiny tremor could be heard in her voice as she spoke.

"He was the kindest person I knew. He always encouraged me when I approached him with any research ideas. It was he who suggested that I explore the assistant professor position that was open in the department. He guided me through the difficult decision to follow my passion for history and archaeological research. He was always there to support me. He was always there to cheer me on." She paused to regain her composure as she recollected in her mind how he had even helped her in relationship matters. "He was like a father to me.

"His childlike curiosity was infectious," she said, a small smile appearing on her face. "'Ree, look what I discovered today'. Ree was what he called me when he was excited about something new.

"He had been excited about a new laser inscription device a few weeks ago. I suspect he inscribed the clue on his bracelet. Though I don't understand how the killers would have known about it."

The three men listened to Reeya intently. They looked at each other to see if anyone had any thoughts about the professor's actions. Being the one with the least knowledge of the background, Kabir started to feel impatient. He was now mentally gearing up to chase after the killers.

"I feel terrible that I didn't give him the opportunity to fully express what was on his mind yesterday," Reeya said, oblivious to the urgency that Kabir was feeling. "He had tried to tell me that I would find the first breadcrumb in this room, should something happen to him," Reeya continued, looking around at the relics.

She regretted interrupting the professor as he mentioned the possibility of someone trying to harm him.

"Nothing will happen to you. We can discuss this tomorrow," she had said, in part to reassure him and in part, as she could not bear the thought of any harm coming to him.

As Reeya gathered her thoughts, Kabir felt it was time to bring in the police force to initiate the process of finding the killer. He took out his phone and made the call. He informed those present in the room that the police would be arriving in just over five minutes.

"You are welcome to stay, but I suspect you'd prefer not to be questioned, at least, not here," Kabir said, in a feeble attempt to suggest that their presence would complicate the investigation.

Taking the hint, Tiwari readied himself to leave. He folded his hands and prayed for the departed soul, then turned to the others. "I'll leave for now, but keep me posted, especially if I can help with anything. The people who killed him seem ruthless. Be safe as you get to the bottom of this."

"Reeya, do you need anything from here to know where the thugs could have gone?" Nair felt that they should get out of there as well. Reeya shook her head and headed to the main door.

"You are both welcome to come to my house as we sort through the clues," Reeya volunteered. "I have some notes from Professor *ji* that may be helpful."

"Kabir can meet us there once he has handed over the investigation to the local police," Nair said. Reeya gave her address and directions to Kabir before heading out.

Kabir was left alone to look around and ponder over his next steps. *What did the professor mean by local furnace? There were several brick kilns in the area—was he talking about one of them? How would they find the one he was referring to? And what's the Giriyak tablet? Giriyak was not far from Rajgir. And where was the last cave?* He knew he'd have to depend on Reeya to decipher the clues.

Kabir stayed just as long as it was necessary after the policemen arrived at the scene. Kabir's second-in-command, ASP Jagdish, was dressed in the khaki uniform of the regular police force. He was a very capable officer. Even though he looked like he was a caricature from a Bollywood movie, he was far from the stereotype. Kabir had come to appreciate the ASP's tenacity in solving cases.

Kabir felt a trifle guilty about withholding crucial background information from the ASP, but he knew so little himself. Apart from what he had learnt from Reeya, there was very little he had to go on. What he needed was for the ASP to gather some hard evidence to help the investigation.

"Jagdish, when I arrived, I found the scene as you see it now. I know you have questions. But for now, I'd ask you to seal the crime scene, dust for prints, and do a thorough forensic scan for any clues you may find," SP Kabir spoke with authority. "Day or night, report any findings directly to me. You know how to reach me."

Kabir looked around one more time. He was trying to commit the scene to memory as he walked through the entry chamber adorned with antiquities. He walked past a policeman in uniform, just outside the porch, who saluted him. A custom leftover from the British colonial times, which was absent-mindedly acknowledged by him with a nod. Kabir stopped at the porch and scanned the surroundings for possible sniper positions.

There was a large mound not far from the professor's house. It was an old, forgotten *stupa*, built around the fifth century BCE, which attracted only the odd tourist now and then. Kabir had spotted a young couple near the stupa just the previous day. They were just standing there, keenly observing their surroundings. He had not thought much about them at that time, but was now wondering if there was a link. The woman, wearing a black choker around her long neck, and the tall man with his hair cropped short seemed to desire the sense of oneness the isolation gave them as they stood there, holding hands, staring into the distance.

The structure and the mound were associated with Ajatshatru,[12] the son of Bimbisara, who founded the Haryanka Dynasty in the sixth-century BCE.[13]. Ajatsatru's reign marks the high watermark of the Sisunaga-Bimbisara dynasty with the political unification of a large part of India.[14]

Instead of his bike, Kabir took one of the jeeps the policeman had got. He drove the jeep as close as possible to the top of the stupa, trying to figure out the best vantage point to the professor's house. The sky was getting lighter as the time for sunrise approached, but Kabir still carried a torch from the jeep. He carefully searched the area, looking between the rocks, around the *stupa*.

A metallic glimmer rewarded his search—a single casing, left behind out of carelessness or maybe in a deliberate gesture of disdain. The sniper was precise. He, or she, had needed just one bullet to do the job. It took a well-trained sniper and a sophisticated rifle to accomplish the task with this precision.

Kabir called Jagdish to update him. "See what more you can find. Get the make and model of the gun, and with any luck, you should be able to locate the source." Kabir hung up and got back into the jeep.

5

Nalanda

Day 1 | 0600 hrs

FOLLOWING THE DIRECTIONS SHE HAD GIVEN, KABIR REACHED Reeya's house. The modest structure and its front yard were enclosed by an iron grill with brick posts, not unlike many others in the area. A local merchant owned the house that had been passed on to him through generations. He and his family lived in the main section located in the front, just a few steps from the unfinished walkway connecting it to the gate.

As Kabir entered the compound, the house help was brooming the yard, clearing it of fallen leaves from the night. Closer to the house, there were string cots, which would have red chillis laid out on them, absorbing the sun to ensure that the monsoon moisture did not spoil them. It was a familiar sight in these parts, where the chillis would end up soaked in oil and pickled to be sold in the local market.

A fork in the driveway led him to the back of the house. A separate brick structure stood there, surrounded by seasonal flowers that were in full bloom. The cheerfully coloured flora in earthen pots painted with intricate designs lined the path.

Kabir knocked at the door, and Nair opened it, letting him in. In sharp contrast to the rustic exterior, the inside was well-appointed with modern furniture and amenities and was neatly kept.

Reeya was crushing some fresh ginger to make tea. "I am assuming you'd want some too. I'm sure you haven't had anything since you woke up," Reeya said.

"Yes. Please," a thankful Kabir replied as he looked around the house. Nair seemed to have made himself comfortable and was reading some notes that Reeya had given him.

"Quite a place you have here," Kabir remarked, surprised at the place that looked more like an apartment in a metropolitan city rather than in rural Rajgir. "I was expecting something more traditional."

"I get that a lot," Reeya said with an amused smile. "Just because I'm a historian-archaeologist, doesn't mean I don't subscribe to modern comforts. Besides, who knows? If our history hadn't been interrupted by invaders, maybe these things would've been designed in India 500 years ago. And today's modern furniture would've been called classical in the present age," she challenged with an impish glint.

Kabir wasn't quite sure how to answer, but he sensed that Reeya's mind was not stuck in bygone ages. Changing the topic, he looked towards Nair and asked, "Anything interesting in that?"

"Yes, actually. It seems our professor had been looking for some clues to solve an ancient mystery. And he did find some. Here, look at this," the deputy chief turned the diary so it would be right way up for Kabir and pushed it in his direction.

Kabir glanced through the diary. Most of the notes were Reeya's, but a couple of sketches were made by the professor, one of which depicted a structure and had an arrow pointing towards a part of it. If they could find that structure, they'd know where to look based on the indicated area. Though it didn't mention what it was they'd be looking for.

"I have seen this somewhere. It will come back to me. Let me give it a thought," Reeya said as she poured the tea and brought out some homemade *nan-khatais* to go with it.

"What do you think he was after?" The question had been on Kabir's mind since he saw the professor's dead body.

"At this point, it's all guesswork," Reeya replied. "Let me give you a brief history for some context."

"It is estimated that Nalanda was founded in the fifth century CE.[15] However, during the excavations, archaeologists have found some cast copper coins from the fourth to the second century BCE,[16] which indicate that it was a thriving town with extensive commerce. There is also evidence that points to Nalanda being functional as a place of learning in the third century BCE. Though further study is needed for that to be verified."

"Either way, that makes Nalanda the oldest residential university on Earth. And since it was operational until at least the 13th century, it is also the longest-running one, spanning a minimum of 800 years.[17] Possibly even 1500 years. It is generally believed that at its peak, Nalanda housed about ten thousand students,[18] and there would be a number of teachers and other visitors residing on campus at any given time. It was the epicentre of higher learning in the known universe, and it attracted students from as far as China and Korea.[19]"

"Of course, Takshila, founded circa the sixth century BCE,[20] or possibly even earlier, is older. But it is not considered a university as it lacks certain essential elements that define a university, like resident students and faculty." Reeya seemed to be enjoying educating them and paused for their reaction.

Kabir was surprised to learn that a two-millennium-old institution, the world's very first university, existed in his own backyard.

"It was a well-planned campus, with over one hundred structures, including several lecture halls. Each one housed the students and faculty that belonged to the department. They were referred to as *viharas*, which somehow got translated to monasteries. Unfortunately, a lot of it seemingly took a religious interpretation in translation. In this case, it may just be because the students lead an austere life, like that of monks.

"We have excavated only eleven of these buildings so far.[21] The rest of the *viharas* remain buried under the village surrounding the site. The Giriyak area is being excavated now." Reeya grew silent as she remembered the professor being at the Giriyak excavation—a likely place to find some answers.

"There were monasteries that we know specialised in advanced medicine, maths, and science. The departments offered further specialisation; the science stream, for example, had metallurgy, astronomy, chemistry, and many others. They also debated philosophy and religion extensively."[22]

Kabir had never felt the urge to visit the ruins before, even though he had known of their existence. But now, as he heard Reeya describe Nalanda, he felt drawn to them. And, perhaps more importantly, he might find a clue to the crime there. The first question that came to him was, "But how did they become ruins?"

Reeya was tempted to ask if he had ever paid attention in his history class. She often felt like that when she found people had grown up without knowing the history of this ancient land. What irked her even more was when some people assumed mythology to be history. She occasionally wondered if ancient Indian history was labelled as mythology by the colonialists, as they did not understand it well.

"Even though Nalanda was the longest-running university, it was not all smooth sailing. Invaders did attack it from time to time, and thrice it saw significant destruction.

"The first time was in the fifth century CE by the Huns under their leader, Mihirakula, after which it wasn't just rebuilt, but also significantly expanded by King Narasimhagupta of the Gupta Dynasty.[23]"

"It was attacked again and at least partially destroyed in the seventh century by the Gauda King Shashanka,[24] to be rebuilt yet again, this time by the King Harshvardhana. He also expanded it and made it even more magnificent.[25] He even invited Chinese scholar Hiuen-Tsang to his assembly to debate along with a thousand monks from Nalanda.[26] Hiuen-Tsang later spent many years in Nalanda before returning to China. He took with him a wealth of knowledge, including 657 manuscripts which he later translated into Chinese.[27] These, no doubt, had a significant impact on Chinese culture.

"Finally, the Turk leader Bakhtiyar Khilji completely destroyed Nalanda around 1205 CE.[28] Records describe the killing of unarmed monks who were tasked with protecting the university.[29] It is estimated that nine million manuscripts were completely charred in the massive conflagration started by him. It burned for so long that even the bricks melted. The melted bricks can still be seen in the remains today.[30]

Figure 2: *Melted Bricks at Nalanda University*

"By the 1500s, the university was just a forgotten ruin. The earth reclaimed what was once its own, and forests and settlements appeared over it. Most of what we know about Nalanda is from records left by students and visitors from far away, including Hiuen-Tsang.[31] It wasn't just the complete destruction of the body of knowledge. It somehow also destroyed the soul of our culture and contributed to its stagnation. I believe that before this incident, our culture had an open mindset, where creativity was encouraged. This was somehow lost in the tragedy and gave way to a more rigid way of thinking.

"Ironically, community and business leaders today are on a quest to rediscover that elusive way of thinking. A growth mindset that questions fixed beliefs. Where curiosity and innovation are respected, and rigour and hard work lead to prosperity. The spirit still exists in our culture, we just need to set it free." Her voice trailed off as she concluded.

By now, Kabir and the deputy chief were completely engrossed in Nalanda's ancient history. There was no impatience in Kabir's voice as he nudged Reeya back to the investigation, "So, where should we start looking for clues?"

Reeya opened her diary to the page that showed the sketch with an arrow indicating a spot. "I didn't realise this before, but this may be the furnace he was mentioning. It would make sense, as it is in the *vihara* for metallurgy, and he is talking about a metal. I know where this building is."

She felt energised as she recognised one of the sketches. "This other structure is—most likely—in the ongoing excavation," she speculated aloud. "Professor *ji* had been spending a lot of time there. It is near the small village of Giriyak. I know the place. I have been there on several occasions. But I didn't know there was a tablet there. I think I needed the *chai* and *nan-khatais* for my mind to start working," she sheepishly admitted with a smile.

"I don't know what 'keep the metal safe' may mean, but the furnace at the ruins is not far from here. I think we should start there," Reeya said, though her face still wore an uncertain expression.

Nair got up and opened a briefcase he had brought with him to Reeya's apartment. "Here, Kabir, I think it is time for you to have these back. I think you will need them."

Kabir recognised his old handgun in its holster. His old wallet with cash in various denominations, credit cards and a few Aadhaar cards. There was also a cell phone, presumably for secure communication.

"I will go and report to the chief. You go and chase after the..."

Kabir interrupted before he could complete, "Were you anticipating something like this when you suggested I relocate to Rajgir, sir?" Kabir had been keeping his curiosity on hold, but could no longer wait to know the exact circumstances behind his transfer.

Nair took a moment before he confessed with a pensive look, "Yes, I did have a feeling that you may be needed here. We had heard some chatter, and I was hoping we'd have more time to investigate and keep the professor safe. We have not established the players or the connections yet, but we are certain that a group of mercenaries have been employed to recover these artefacts from wherever they may now be. I will keep you informed of any further developments. Right now, finding those artefacts is of paramount importance. The professor believed that they were a clue to a scientific process that has great value today. As you know, nuclear reaction was mentioned, which is why we are involved. It seems improbable, but we must explore the possibility." He wished Reeya and Kabir luck as he bid farewell.

Reeya filled a bottle of water and was picking up some snacks when Kabir asked, "What is that for? The Nalanda ruins are just thirty minutes away."

"What if I get thirsty or hungry?" Reeya said, sounding like a Girl Scout who was prepared for any contingency.

Kabir sighed, and for a moment remembered Vani, who would have done the same.

6
Giriyak

Day 1 | 0730 hrs

IT WAS QUITE EARLY IN THE MORNING WHEN THEY REACHED THE ruins. The cool air and the expanse of grass caused a mist to shroud the ruins. The rising sun would dissipate it later in the day. For now, it gave the place an eerie look.

The guard allowed the police jeep to pass through after the requisite identification check. A long, solitary path led to the ruins and then curved over to the end of the excavated monasteries. Reeya gave directions to the furnace, and Kabir parked a few yards away from it. For a moment, Kabir just stood there imagining what the university would have looked like in its prime. He visualised a majestic compound, with several multi-storeyed *viharas*. And the furnace would have been in a bustling state-of-the-art laboratory of the ancient world.

"The nucleus of the university was the nine-storied library building,"[32] Reeya explained. Kabir could envision the monks taking a stroll on the campus with the central building touching the clouds. He imagined an emissary of the king galloping in on a horse bearing a message or an inquiry for the scholars.

"Do you have a shovel in that metal box you call a jeep?" she asked, mocking the vehicle that lacked even a music player.

Kabir smiled as he understood her frustration, drawing a parallel with Vani again. *How similar in thought the two are!* He found a steel rod that could be used as a crowbar—it would have to do for now.

The one-foot-high stub of the furnace was all that could be seen, making an X, each leg about thirty feet long. Each of the resulting angles was bulged out to make a chamber. Each of the four chambers of the smelting furnace had two channels, acting as flues.[33] The irony of looking for a clue in this large X was not lost on Reeya.

Figure 3: *X-shaped furnace at Nalanda University*

She took out the diary, turned to the page with the sketch and aligned it to the furnace. Kabir hesitated as he knew that it was a cognizable offence to disturb a historic site. Yet he felt that he had no option but to dig to find some clues. He bent his head to find that someone had recently dug at a spot. He wondered if it was the professor who had hidden something there. He took the crowbar and dug at the disturbed location. Almost immediately, he struck a metal piece and brought it out. Despite the dirt clinging to it, Reeya could tell it didn't belong there.

Reeya examined the piece in her hands and then used the water in her bottle to wash off the dirt. It had a dark grey metallic lustre with a fine pattern, like wood grains. The concave shape of the metal suggested it was a fragment of something larger, perhaps something spherical in shape. Reeya gasped. She had studied it and seen it in pictures, but had not thought that such a metal was used to make anything other than swords or knives.

"It's a wootz steel fragment," she said. "I think. I've not seen it as a fragment before, but this is wootz for sure."

Expecting that Kabir would want to know more, she continued, "This was a type of steel that was made in southern India, which has a rich history of scientific achievement, including in the field of metallurgy. There are several legends that talk about its mystical qualities. What is more interesting is that this was likely the very first kind of steel that was produced applying a process to control the carbide morphology."[34]

Sensing that it was getting too technical for Kabir, Reeya focused on its history instead. "It was in great demand, especially in the Middle East and by cultures that used it to make weapons.[35] South India[36] was the birthplace of high-carbon steel, made in industrial-size batches to be exported to Damascus and other places as ingots.[37] I'm sure you have heard of Damascus steel."[38]

Kabir stared back blankly. "I thought steel was made in the mid-1800s by someone called Bessemer, who was knighted for inventing the process."

Reeya was not surprised at Kabir's lack of awareness on the subject. She lamented that a lot of the ancient history had not been properly preserved or recorded. And what little was known may have been moulded to suit the narrative of the conquerors of a past era. She reflected on how the wootz production slowly died when the British government banned it in the 18th century CE.[39]

The curiosity to discover and share long-forgotten truths was what drove her to be a historian-archaeologist. Kabir was gradually learning the burning passion that lingered under the gentle demeanour.

"The technology needed to facilitate both the production and processing of wootz[40] has been discovered in various locations. One of the sites, Kodumanal in Tamil Nadu, dates back to the third century BCE.[41] But first, we must hurry to the site of the excavation in Giriyak for the next clue." It was clear Reeya realised time was of the essence.

She held the piece of cold steel in her hands with a reverence that seemed appropriate to its mysteriousness. The pattern on the steel shimmered in the morning sunlight just like ocean waves. Reeya realised that this fragment of steel could be anywhere from a few hundred to two thousand years old.

"Let's head to the Giriyak excavation site now. I know where it is. It will take us about half an hour. Hopefully a little less at this hour," Reeya said, carefully keeping the wootz fragment in her bag as she got into the police vehicle.

Reeya's mind wandered to the bracelet the murderers took off the Professor's wrist. *I wonder what was inscribed on it? Could it have some clues that would give them a head start?*

Day 1 | 0930 hrs

Following Reeya's directions, Kabir drove to the site in good time. It was a beautiful drive now that the green hills were becoming more visible, with the mist lingering only at the peaks.

Reeya was examining the wootz fragment they had dug up for any clues it might hold. Beautiful as the shimmering grains looked, she was not able to learn much from them. Entering the excavation site, they noticed there was no guard on duty. Reeya saw a fallen chair and a body near it and looked at Kabir with fear in her eyes. Kabir saw it too and stopped the vehicle on the side of the deserted road, and they sprinted to the guard who was lying with his hands and feet expertly tied. As Kabir undid the ropes, he questioned the guard about what had happened. The guard, still in a daze, tried to explain.

"They came in a black SUV from that side," pointing to the road where Kabir and Reeya had just come from. A rather futile piece of information, as that was the only entry to the site.

"She pointed a gun at me, and I just froze. A man with her came and tied me up. I tried to scream, but no sound came out." The guard, stammering, with wide eyes as though he saw a ghost, was trying to recover his wits. Kabir tried to calm him down so that he could get some useful information.

"They had guns and they looked dangerous," the guard continued, somewhat incoherently, as he tried to recall more details. "They were foreigners. They were speaking in a language I didn't know. Not English. The woman was giving orders to search for something."

Reeya brought him some water. The guard was thankful for the gesture as he gulped it down. It seemed to revive him somewhat, and he got to his feet.

Some clarity of thought seemed to have returned to the guard. "As I lay tied up on my stomach, I could see they were shovelling, searching for something. They found what looked like a piece of a stone tablet. I think they were trying to read the inscription on it." With a frown as he recalled, the guard continued, "Oddly, I noticed the professor looking at something similar yesterday. Normally, he takes such excavated objects with him to the university for cataloguing. But yesterday, he put it back and covered it with dirt. I did not think much of it at the time. But I think it was the same broken stone tablet. Yes, it was a pink stone, squarish, about one foot on each side. And it seemed broken on one end and rounded on the other."

Kabir gave Reeya a quizzical look. She nodded in response and then spoke softly, "We must assume that they came for the broken tablet and found it. Again, I am not sure how they found out, but I assume it may have been what the professor had inscribed on his bracelet." With regret in her voice, she continued, "They seem to be a step ahead of us."

She considered the mystical grey metal she had with her and corrected herself, "Well, at least they are ahead of us in that they know what is on the tablet, and we don't. If we want to catch up, we need to find the thugs."

Sensing Reeya's determination, Kabir gave her a reassuring smile and said, "We don't know how to find them yet. But we will."

The site extended to an open terrace. It had been neatly cleared of debris except for where the tablet seemed to have been. Reeya spent some time looking into the rubble, hoping to find some clues to what may have been on the tablet. Or even, if she was lucky, the other half.

But her search didn't yield anything. She was convinced that only one half of the tablet had been placed there, perhaps deliberately. *But by whom?* The guard did not remember any other visitor to the site.

Reeya was kicking herself for not coming to Giriyak first. They had missed the opportunity to get ahead of the mercenaries, who seemed as determined as they themselves were to discover this secret that the centuries had hidden.

Sensing her mentally chiding herself, Kabir said, "I am glad we went to the other site and found the mystery wootz first," putting a comical emphasis on the word *wootz.*

She nodded, understanding the futility of doubting herself. Kabir was right—if they had come here first, they would still not have made it in time. At least now they knew something that the other group did not—the existence of the concave fragment of wootz.

The sun was nearly overhead, and even though it was monsoon, they could feel the scorching heat. Without the fog or cloud cover, it was getting difficult to stand in the middle of the excavation site.

Reeya turned to Kabir and said, "We should head to Udaygiri as quickly as we can. I am sure they haven't connected the dots yet, but they will eventually figure out its importance."

Reeya felt a sense of panic rise within her as she thought of those ruthless killers having been at Giriyak before them. Worse yet, they could still be lurking around somewhere right now!

7

Udaygiri

Day 1 | 1200 hrs

KABIR ACCEPTED REEYA'S DECISION WITHOUT QUESTIONING IT. Being in sync with her sense of urgency, he signalled to her to proceed towards the jeep, as he called the deputy chief on the secure handset that he had been given.

"Any chance of getting us transport to Udaygiri?"

"Yes, in Madhya Pradesh, near Bhopal?"

"Yes."

Reeya could hear only one side of the conversation as she sat buckled in the jeep.

"A plane will be waiting for us at the Patna airport to take us to Udaygiri," Kabir informed Reeya after finishing his call to Nair. "How did you figure out that the next place we need to go to is Udaygiri?" asked Kabir curiously. "Was there a clue I missed?"

"Remember the professor's note at the back of the painting? It pointed us to the iron pillar and the last cave. Now, most people would automatically think of the iron pillar in the Qutub Minar complex in Delhi. It is believed to be the oldest iron pillar in the world and an exemplary achievement in the field of metallurgy.[42] The pillar, though seated in Delhi for about eight hundred years, has been in existence for much longer.[43] And yet it shows almost no signs of corrosion.

"Let's go with the assumption that these thugs also know of this pillar. Logically, they should be headed to Delhi right now," she continued. "I don't think many people know that the pillar was not originally erected in Delhi. The professor's note provides us with a clear clue. The iron pillar was originally erected in Udaygiri, and there is a series of caves where it was first installed."[44]

Kabir felt somewhat guilty about not having known the origin of the iron pillar. He, too, had thought of Delhi at the mention of the iron pillar.

Kabir swerved the jeep to avoid some goats in the middle of the road, which had separated from their herd. One had to be very attentive driving on the two-lane 'highway' meandering through the farmlands of India. Domestic animals often occupied the roads as if they had been specifically built for their convenience!

Kabir wanted to stop to get some *chai* from a roadside *dhaba*—rustic eateries for truckers along highways. It was tempting to forget everything for a moment and sit in the open air under a large extended canopy and get some food. The *dhabas* were known for their simple yet flavourful and cheap fare.

Mirroring his thoughts, Reeya said, "Would have loved some *chai* and *pakoras*, but I think we have to hurry, right?"

Kabir smiled as he thought about how easily Reeya seemed to read his mind.

Reeya was quite familiar with Patna. Both by virtue of it being the capital of Bihar—the state she lived in—and because of its rich history. Pataliputra, as it was known at its inception around the fifth century BCE,[45] became the capital of the Maurya Empire.[46] By the third century BCE, it was the largest city in the world.[47] New evidence being unearthed, literally, may indicate a settlement could've existed even earlier.

Patna was a vibrant city. Its streets were crowded as usual at this hour. The colours and noise assaulted the senses. Horns blared as vehicles weaved through the traffic. Street vendors flanked either side of the road, with large signs proclaiming their wares to be the best. Reeya realised she was hungry at the sight of the hawkers' stalls selling mouthwatering local dishes.

Her mind was making a noise of its own with thoughts racing faster than the cars on the road. She tried to dull that and focus on what to expect in Udaygiri. It had been a while since she had visited the place.

Kabir drove past the airport building towards the back of the airport. The uniformed guard at the entrance of the hangar area gave him a brisk salute after he showed his ID. As he parked the jeep near the rear entrance of what looked like a research facility, Reeya looked confused.

"We use this back gate for VIPs or emergencies. We will find our plane waiting for us just a short walk away," Kabir said, leading the way.

Reeya had never flown privately before but had certainly seen private jets in movies. She tried to appear nonchalant, as if she knew what was going on. As they jogged to the plane, Reeya was glad that she had chosen to wear sensible shoes with all the walking she had done since the morning.

She had expected a luxurious private jet to be waiting for them, with opulent interiors and reclining seats, but as she entered the plane with old-fashioned propellers, what she found was a basic 16-seater with only the necessities. Reluctantly, she looked around for any signs that something might come apart and break.

"It's a government-issue plane. There may not be food on board, but we will reach safely in about two hours. Pick any seat and make yourself comfortable," Kabir tried reassuring her.

Finding a seat in the mid-section of the plane, Reeya made herself comfortable. She took off her shoes and put her legs on the seat, massaging her feet. Kabir came and sat across the aisle from her.

Once they were airborne, Reeya brought out some snacks from her bag. She was thankful that there was at least a bottle of water at every seat. She offered some of the snacks to Kabir, who, after a bit of hesitation, accepted the peanuts thankfully.

As the plane reached cruising altitude, Kabir wanted to know more details about their destination. Still munching on the peanuts, he leaned over the aisle between them and asked. "What is so special about Udaygiri? What are we expecting to find there?"

Reeya turned her notebook and started to draw at a tilted angle so he could see what she was sketching—a map of Udaygiri. "Udaygiri was a major astronomical observatory in ancient India. Studies regarding the heavenly bodies were conducted here even before the Gupta dynasty.[48] Vidisha, about sixty kilometres north-east of Bhopal, was situated at the junction of ancient trade routes and enjoyed a good deal of economic progress.[49]

"Here," said Reeya, as she pointed to the map. "About ten kilometres away from Vidisha is Udaygiri. It was a suburb of Vidisha back in the day, and where Delhi's Iron Pillar was originally erected.[50] We will need to go to the last cave, which, if memory serves me right, is cave number twenty. It is located at the furthest end[51] from the entrance to the Udaygiri caves complex."

"But why was the iron pillar erected in such a complex?" Kabir asked, his curiosity piqued.

Reeya paused and seemed to be considering which point in history she should rewind so that it would be easy for Kabir to understand.

"Well, there could be multiple reasons for it," she continued. "The first question we must ask is, why make a pillar like that at all! It is not like a few farmer friends woke up one morning with a startup idea of making a six-ton, seven-and-a-half-meter tall pillar[52] in their backyard that hasn't rusted yet.

"Based on the findings and nearby monuments, we can assume that there was a sizeable ironsmith community in the area, and they were making high-quality iron as far back as the fifth-fourth century BCE or even earlier[53], making the region that spans all the way south to Sri Lanka the first to have large scale iron production.

"The answer to 'why at this location' is more interesting. We know that the inhabitants of the area were well-versed not just in metallurgy but also in astronomy. The iron pillar was erected in such a way that the shadow of the top of the pillar touched the feet of the deities in each of the major caves on the day of the summer solstice. It is also interesting that the pillar was installed at a point where the Tropic of Cancer would have passed at that time.[54] The Tropic has shifted somewhat southwards since then."

Day 1 | 1600 hrs

Once the plane came to a stop in a remote corner of the airport, the pilot came out of the cockpit, opened the door and pushed out the airstair for them to disembark.

The evening sun was still warm, burning their skin even through the sweat-soaked clothes that now clung to their bodies, but the occasional shade of a passing cloud provided much-needed relief. Kabir saw an army jeep nearby with the deputy chief standing next to it. Instinctively, he knew something was not right. There was no reason for Nair to be here. Whatever he had to communicate, they could have done so over their secure devices.

"Sir?" Kabir looked at him with a nod.

"Kabir, here are the photos of those we believe are responsible for the professor's murder." Nair pulled out some pictures from a brown envelope. "These were taken earlier today at the Delhi airport as passengers from a flight from

Patna deplaned. Airport security had been alerted to look out for anyone suspicious, and they picked out these four passengers. We cross-checked their seating and identity. They hold passports from various European nations and travelled in separate parts of the plane.

"However, soon after, the cameras captured this picture. There must've been some emergency as the group seems to have thrown caution to the wind and come together to discuss something within the airport," continued the deputy chief as he showed them a picture of three men and a woman huddled together.

Nair proceeded to show them mug shots of each of the participants. "We know them to be mercenaries. And this one is their leader—Myra," said the deputy chief, holding up the picture of a woman.

"We have been tracking their activities for a while now, and believe they represent a powerful and well-funded organisation that is after a historical artefact."

Kabir recognised Myra as the tourist with the black choker he had seen on the Ajatshatru Stupa the previous day. He also recognised the man with short, cropped hair as one of her accomplices.

"After their meeting, they exited the airport separately, but soon after, they all bought plane tickets to Bhopal. We did not stop them as we wanted to track their activities." This statement from the deputy chief alarmed Kabir.

"Are you saying we have a mole?" It was a reasonable assumption given that the mercenary group had deciphered the next clue. "We knew to come here because Reeya knew the origin of the iron pillar." Kabir proceeded to tell Nair what Reeya had told him.

"Kabir, only a handful of people knew you were coming here. And each person on this team has been carefully vetted. I am not sure how they could have found out," Nair was just as puzzled.

It was plausible that the mercenaries had headed to the generally known location of the pillar, but then had to revise their plans as they dug deeper to determine where the pillar was first erected. It could have been a simple internet search, but Nair could not shake off the possibility of a mole from his mind.

Nair handed the envelope and pictures to Kabir, along with a stacked steel lunch box, saying, "Oh, and here. Vani's mom sent this tiffin. She insisted I take it with me when I told her that I'd be meeting you. I'm sure you could both do with a home-cooked meal."

Referring to one's spouse as the mother or father of their child was customary when talking to friends and family. Kabir felt a sense of belonging when the deputy chief referred to his wife as Vani's mom.

"How has she been holding up?" Kabir asked. Even though they were in a hurry, he knew that taking a few extra minutes to enquire about her well-being would not impact the schedule.

"She is strong," Nair said with a sigh and a forced momentary smile. "She misses Vani and has her moments.

"Reeya *bete*, make sure you both eat well," the deputy chief had taken a liking to Reeya. Perhaps he, too, saw some of Vani's qualities in her.

"And Kabir, use the secure mobile if you need to, but let's assume that we may not be the only ones listening in," cautioned Nair as Kabir and Reeya turned towards the camouflage-painted jeep.

Kabir identified the two men who came with the jeep as part of the Reserve Forces, seeing the insignia on their uniforms. The driver was clean-shaven and wearing dark glasses. The other had a muscular body and sported a closely trimmed beard. He introduced himself as Pratap, and the driver as Anand, as he greeted Kabir and held open the back door for them to get in.

Reeya was famished and was already opening the lunch box as she settled down. She laid out the containers in the small space between them.

It was the first time they were sitting close to each other. Kabir liked the confidence and energy with which she had taken the lead to guide them through their search. But this was the first time he saw Reeya as a person and not just a source of knowledge.

She generously offered some food to the men sitting in the front, but they politely declined. Kabir noticed she was giving him a larger portion—a caring gesture on her part. As they finished their food, she stacked away the steel containers. Her kind and thoughtful gestures made Kabir feel a sense of warmth towards her.

He was curious about her, "You don't seem to be native to Rajgir. How did you end up there?"

Reeya laughed, confessing, "I was going to ask you the same thing."

He had been very open and had respected her opinion as an equal. She had felt valued as she provided direction to their investigation. Looking into his eyes, something told her that she could confide in him.

"I wanted to understand our ancient history and culture. I feel there is a lot that has not been looked at objectively," she said in answer to his question.

Then pausing, as she often did, to gather her thoughts, Reeya said, "Let's just say, while growing up, I did not really know how old our civilisation was. Not having clear evidence of when, for example, the *Vedas* or the *Mahabharat* were composed, and how long were they transmitted orally from one generation to the next before they were written. It all got me curious.

"The more I studied the subject, the more I realised that we view our history from a Eurocentric perspective. While textbooks today may include much more, I wasn't aware of a lot of things growing up. We have cave drawings from 8000 BCE[55] and what now seems to be a continuous civilisation from even before 5000 BCE. After the first Harappan site was discovered in the early 1920s, exploration and surveys have found more than 2000 sites of that civilisation or its affiliates in the Indian sub-continent. Of these, Gujarat alone accounts for over 550[56] populated towns that we won't know much about until we excavate them. In all likelihood, there are many more that still need to be discovered.

"aDNA samples taken from human skeletal remains from Indus Valley sites show a robust match with various ethnic groups that form our current population, pointing to a continued civilisation[57]. As we now use modern scientific methods to stitch through the gaps that we have seen in history in the past, we will get a realistic view of how our languages and culture grew and spread. I feel it will make our thinking more objective." Reeya seemed to have drifted with her thoughts as she gazed past him.

Kabir was listening intently. He liked how she was able to quickly summarise the history that he had missed out in school.

"I must not have paid attention to my teachers in ninth grade," he confided with a sheepish grin. "But it also sounds like you are a bit of a revisionist, or perhaps a nationalist," continued Kabir with a little laugh. He did not mean to assign a label, but to provoke a response.

The jeep had made it to the newly built highway towards Udaygiri. It passed some construction areas that will eventually make it easier to get there, but for now, it was prudent to pass through Vidisha. The smoothness of the highway gave way to a riot of potholes that threw the passengers in every direction. A row of shops with bright signs and a tangle of power lines announced that they are now passing through the town of Vidisha.

Ignoring the change in the scenery, Reeya laughed too with Kabir and with a smile, continued, "Yes, I suppose you could call me that. Though I can assure you that what I have found so far will not necessarily please the nationalists either."

She decided it was not the place or venue to elaborate on her opinions about equal rights, security, and freedom for women to live their lives as they saw fit. She suppressed her urge to discuss that women in ancient times had the freedom to wear 'not-too-modest' clothes, as depicted in temple statues. Or how the *Arthashastra* has a full chapter dedicated to the consumption and taxation of meat and alcohol.[58]

"Actually, it is not that I'm a revisionist. I merely try to make sure we can explain what we observe in a rational manner. Let me give you an example." She decided it was probably a good way to illustrate what she did as a historian.

"We all know of Alexander, the Greek conqueror from Macedonia, who had set out to expand his reign. In Persia, he was perhaps known as Alexander the Destroyer as he razed Persepolis, the Persian capital,[59] and destroyed the temples of the Zoroastrians. Greece had a prominent position in the Western narrative, and so it can be seen why he is known as Alexander 'the Great' instead."

Kabir noticed the increased intensity in her tone as she continued. "Either way, it is established that, driven by India's wealth at the time, Alexander planned to invade it largely to monopolise the trade routes, including the ports, and to use his military might to control the commercial resources of ancient India, making India his prized objective.[60]

"After destroying Persia, his forces marched ahead to their stated objective. He reached the river Jhelum (known as *Hydaspes* to the Greeks)[61] and stopped there, in awe of the formidable army that confronted them. In the Greek narrative, Alexander defeated the forces of Porus—the ruler of

Punjab—at Jhelum, and returned to Greece, after re-crowning Porus as King."[62] Reeya took a pause to see if Kabir was still engaged.

"Well, for a conqueror—who raided and destroyed several civilisations, looted several tons of gold from Persia, to have reached the land famous for its riches, wage a bloody battle, where he lost several of his generals and close associates, and then just pack up and leave—does not make sense," Reeya said it all in one breath.

"While this is the Greek version, the little that has survived elsewhere does not suggest that Alexander succeeded or that there was a battle at all! Again, absence of evidence does not mean an event did not occur, but does make you question it." Reeya was now ready to defend her approach as a historian. "Call me revisionist if you will, but as a historian, we must make conclusions based on recorded evidence across civilisations. After exhaustive investigation, if it causes history to be rewritten, then so be it."

Kabir was not sure if it was the passion with which she spoke or the rational argument she had put forward that left him mesmerised. Either way, he found he enjoyed listening to her.

"As we find more artefacts, are we to expect that there will be further revisions to recorded history?" It was all Kabir could think of saying, in an attempt to show his interest in the subject.

Reeya decided to answer the question with a little background. "I met the Professor when he was visiting the UK, where I was studying before I returned to India. I was impressed with his approach. He was using hard evidence, like artefacts and written records, to separate myth from fact, religion and mythology from history, to ensure history hadn't been misinterpreted.

"I jumped at the opportunity when he offered me a guest lectureship. It aligned with my passion to examine history objectively. So, to answer your question, yes. As we continue to separate myth from facts, history will need to be continuously revised," She concluded.

While all that she said was true, she didn't tell Kabir the other reason for her coming away to Rajgir. She was still not ready to tell him about Arjun. She wasn't sure herself if the real reason she had followed the professor back to India was her passion for history or wanting to get away from Arjun.

Arjun was a successful businessman settled in the UK. He came from a wealthy family and had been groomed to take over the business someday. She did like him and had put in effort into the relationship in hopes of finding a spark. But she had not felt valued, and just could not see herself conform to the lifestyle he had envisioned for her. She was determined to do something meaningful with her life and was convinced that Arjun's possessiveness and fixed mindset would not allow her to blossom.

"Do you think that the professor found something that was going to rewrite the past?" Kabir understood that certain discoveries could fundamentally change how we look at history.

"Maybe we can find the tons of gold that Alexander took from Persia?" Kabir said in jest.

"Let's just follow the leads we have and see where it takes us," Reeya said, trained to avoid the pitfalls of jumping to conclusions.

"And, by the way, my hypothesis is that Alexander saw the military might of Porus and never conquered any part of India." She smiled as she added, "It would explain why he never took any gold from India and returned with just a hundred talents, or about three tons of steel, that was gifted to him.[63] If he had won, I'm sure he would have had more to show for it."

The conversation made the long drive go by quickly. As it was, the lush green trees lining the smooth new highway and the crops in the farms on either side made for a very soothing and comfortable ride. The staple roadside *dhabas* infused colour with their bright awnings into the shades of greens that stretched as far as the eye could see.

As they entered Vidisha, they had to negotiate the crowded main street with shops and street vendors on both sides. Stretched for time, they swept past all the tourist haunts to avoid getting delayed. The smooth highway gave way to a bumpy street for a few kilometres. Reeya was grateful that the bumpy ride had started after the food had settled in their stomachs. Finally, they left the colourful and noisy markets behind and drove on to the tree-lined road leading to the Udaygiri caves.

The green foliage acquired a rich golden hue in the setting sun. Kabir and Reeya were aware of the beauty of their surroundings as they continued their discussion, but chose to stay focused on the task at hand. For an instant, as their eyes locked, they wished they were seeing the sunset under different circumstances.

"Maybe another day," Kabir thought aloud. Reeya smiled and nodded.

They reached just as the monument was shutting down to visitors for the day. Kabir's credentials and the army vehicle they were in ensured that the guard raised no objections to their entry.

Pratap stepped out, allowing Reeya and Kabir to exit the vehicle. "The rest of the journey will have to be done on foot," he said in characteristic staccato army style as he went towards the back of the vehicle. "Let me get some torches as it will get dark soon," Pratap continued while gesturing to Anand to stay with the vehicle.

"Where are you headed?" enquired the guard at the gate.

Kabir was still deciding if he wanted to answer the question when Reeya spoke, "Last cave. Cave 20."

The guard nodded and said, "It has been closed to the public for a long time. It will be full of bats and wasps. I would not suggest going there unprepared at this hour."

Seeing clearly from Kabir's face that they would be going in, regardless, the guard started thinking of how he could help.

"Give me a minute," he said as he went into his cabin.

He came back with a large metal ring holding several dozen keys. He sorted through them and took out the one that opened Cave 20. Kabir took the key and thanked the guard, knowing he was bending the rules for him.

"Based on when Myra and her crew landed in Delhi, I think we have under two hours to get out of here. Unless we want to catch sniper fire on our way back," he said. "Given the urgency of the situation, I'm sure they won't wait for the next commercial flight. They would have found a faster way."

Although Kabir had memorised the sketch that Reeya had drawn on the plane, indicating the location of the last cave, she led the way with him and Pratap following.

Reeya seemed to be enjoying playing the guide. The role play seemed to keep her fears and anxieties at bay.

"These caves are generally said to have been cut around 400 CE[64], or perhaps earlier, and they contain what is probably the oldest surviving Hindu and Jain iconography,[65]" she said enthusiastically.

As they continued to move past several caves, Reeya continued, "I find this one very interesting, and I would like to visit it to study in greater detail sometime. It has a Shiva Linga that is carved along with his Asta-Shakti, the eight females.[66] As you may know, Ling and Yoni are the two opposite halves that make a whole. Some think the idea travelled to China along with Buddhism and became better known as Yin and Yang. A similar concept."

Reeya carried on, without realising that Kabir found her absent-minded commentary both enchanting and amusing. "The door frame of this cave also has several musical instruments, including, it seems, a lute, and an instrument that resembles a guitar.[67] Yeah, in the 4th or early 5th century CE."[68]

They now reached what seemed like a naturally formed auditorium. There were caves and sculptures on both sides, with some large carved-out alcoves. It was a fascinating place and made one wonder what stories it had to tell.

Reeya pointed downwards from there, to a spot roughly outside the boundary wall, to the other side of the adjoining street, visible from the 'auditorium'. "That's generally believed to be the spot where Delhi's iron pillar was originally installed."

Kabir was taking in the scene as they climbed higher, looking down at the city below. The greenery stretched to the horizon with the last of the golden rays just before sunset still illuminating their path.

Kabir instinctively looked down for any approaching vehicle that could be carrying Myra and her team. For now, he saw nothing that alarmed him, but he knew they needed to keep moving and be vigilant.

They were soon reaching the top of the 350-feet-high hill. They walked past a guest house constructed of brick and stone with a pediment that did not fit in with the natural surroundings. It was built by the British as a weekend cottage for high-ranking officers or those who could afford to pay for the view, but now sat vacant and abandoned.

A place to hide if we need to, Kabir made a mental note of it, as he ran various scenarios through his mind, in case the enemy caught up with them.

Continuing up the ancient stone steps, they reached a flat rock top from where they could see the adjoining farms, forest and river. There was a dam across the river, and they could hear the cascading water, blending with the chirping of birds and insects.

Kabir snapped back to the present and started thinking about how not to get stung by the bees and wasps once inside the cave. He decided it would be a good idea to build a fire to smoke out the critters. The rainy season had made the underbrush moist, but he found some relatively dry twigs he could use.

Kabir saw a small cabin for the guard near the doorway to the cave. Peeking into it for more material for his fire, he wondered why someone would design a modern structure with glass windows right next to a heritage cave.

He was glad to find an old newspaper in the cabin. With the items secured under his arm, he proceeded to open the lock of Cave 20. The key was a bit hard to turn, but a small jiggle and Kabir had the door open.

Having climbed up to the top of the hill to reach the gate, they now looked at the stairs leading down several floors. It was warm, humid, and dark. Pratap turned up the torchlight to reflect the beam off the ceiling, bathing the stairwell in an ambient glow. The moisture in the air was now accompanied by a stale smell which the cool monsoon winds did little to relieve.

Kabir bundled the twigs carefully in the newspaper and, taking a match from Pratap, lit the pile, carefully descending a few steps before tossing the smoke bomb as far down as he could. He gestured to the other two to quickly retreat as the flames grew and the smoke started to spread. The loud buzzing sounds of bees gave them a sense of urgency as they rushed back out of the cave, climbing the steep steps as quickly as they could.

"Hurry up and get into the guard's cabin!" Kabir instructed.

The buzzing increased as the bees and wasps came out in the thousands just as the trio rushed into the cabin. Kabir picked up some more sticks and, wrapping them in newspaper, set them on fire. Carrying the makeshift torch, he braved it to the entrance to smoke away the bees from their only access into the cave.

Seeing the buzzing subside, Reeya thought it safe to approach the door. But as she got closer, she saw a thousand shimmering eyes, coming at her screeching. The cloud of bats also wanted to escape the smoke in the cave.

Reeya screamed at the sight of the creatures coming towards her. She instinctively turned towards Kabir and buried her face in his shoulder. Without a thought other than Reeya's safety, Kabir held her and turned around to swerve away from the black flying swarm.

The flurry of activity stopped as the insects and bats cleared the cave. Reeya took an extra moment before she emerged from Kabir's shoulder. She had felt safe and comforted by his smell and how he held her. She looked up, and Kabir smiled back as she adjusted her glasses that had been dislodged. A silent, yet implicit communication acknowledged the moment that had transpired between them.

With her eyeglasses back in place and regaining her composure, Reeya once again moved towards the steps leading down into the cave. The two men followed her into the narrow stairwell, which was now full of smoke. It was difficult to breathe, and they waved their hands in front to clear the air.

The action was having little effect, as Reeya soon realised. Her eyes started to water, and beads of sweat formed on her brow with the heat.

They descended about the depth of two floors and reached a vestibule leading to a large rectangular room divided into five parts. The torches lit up various objects and inscriptions. Reeya pointed hers to a saintly figure sitting under a serpent hood—all carved in stone.

"That is the statue of Tirthankara.[69] He is a central figure in the Jain religion. Of the twenty caves here, this one is decidedly a Jain cave. The religions used to coexist from about fifth century BCE. But I doubt this is what we are looking for. We need to find something that does not belong here." Reeya had a casual way of informing while at the same time eliciting cooperation.

Kabir and Pratap moved their torches around as they marvelled at the antiquities and ancient scripts in the chamber, not knowing exactly how they would find what did not belong there.

"There is an excavated section in the room on the south," Reeya said softly, mostly to herself, as if she did not want to disturb the silence.

She pushed her way towards where she thought the room was. There in the southern room, even before reaching the remains of the excavation, she spotted an earthen urn-like object.

Reeya proceeded towards the brinjal-shaped object, as she cleared the imaginary as well as real cobwebs in the heavy air in front of her. Kabir had never seen anything like the fired clay object before them. It was the size of a large bottle of champagne with a narrow neck and rounded belly.

Kabir and Pratap exchanged blank looks as they turned to face Reeya again.

"We historians refer to it as a retort," she said and seeing the confused faces of the two, she continued. "A similarly shaped vessel is used commonly in distillation processes even today. The neck of this one is broken, so it is hard to say what it was used for."

She continued examining the brinjal-shaped object closely. Holding it firmly, she shook it and shone her torchlight inside the broken neck to see if there was anything inside.

"But it does not belong here. This type of baked retort was used many centuries ago, mostly in the Rajasthan area[70]. It was obviously brought here, though I don't know why. Judging from its condition, it seems to have been untouched for a long time, possibly centuries," she thought aloud.

Reeya continued to clear the centuries-old dust off the object as she held it rather reverentially. Pratap volunteered a handkerchief, trying to be of some help. Reeya exchanged her torch for the handkerchief and asked him to illuminate the object while she carefully proceeded to dust it.

Soon, she was able to detect some markings on the object. Continuing to clear it expertly, she was able to discern that they were etched onto it, perhaps with a sharp object. The etching was not baked onto the retort but was added later. Reeya cleaned the object a little more and adjusted the angle so the torchlight illuminated it better. She could make out the drawing as something she had seen before—the Heliodorus Pillar.

"*Garuda*," Reeya recognised the form on top of the capital. *Garuda* was part human-part bird, and was referred to in ancient Indian scriptures.

"The Heliodorus column does not have the *Garuda* capital on it today. But this is the pillar when it was intact. We don't know when or how the capital was broken or lost, but we do know it had *Garuda* as the capital."

While Reeya filled the two men in on what she saw, she was still wondering why the image was drawn on the retort. Brushing it as she turned the retort in her hands, she saw some other markings as well. There were three lines of short and long dashes, almost like Morse code, with the sequence of each line interrupted by a vertical line.

"Kabir, this makes no sense to me. Here is a retort with an image resembling a pillar etched on one side and what looks like Morse code on the other. I'm sure the image is that of the Heliodorus Pillar—that is, the pillar as it was before the capital broke off. So, we can assume it was etched many centuries ago," Reeya explained her bafflement. "But I'm not sure what the Morse code-like inscription is and what this has to do with the Professor's death."

"Let me decipher the Morse code. Maybe then we can figure out what it's doing on the retort?" Kabir said helpfully.

"It resembles Morse code, but I don't think it actually is," Reeya said, reading the dashes and the dots out loud. "The sequence is --- --- | --- - ---"

Kabir was just as puzzled by the mysterious code. He was also starting to worry about the mercenaries on their tail. He turned towards Pratap and said softly, "We are almost done here. You should go up and keep a watch.

"Reeya, can you see anything else which may be of importance as a clue?" Kabir figured it would be prudent to pick up any other item that seemed like it could help them in their quest and get the hell out.

As Kabir shone his torch around the cave, Reeya looked around but could not see much else that could be of value. She decided to take a video and some pictures of the inscriptions and carvings on the walls to refer to later.

The smoke had cleared out, and the bees and wasps seemed to be returning home. Dodging them, Kabir and Reeya went up the narrow stairs. She kept stopping to take as many photos as she could of the statues and wall carvings that they passed.

On exiting, Kabir locked the door and they sprinted back up the naturally formed stone steps, now illuminated by the moonlight and the light of the torches they carried.

As they reached the top, Kabir instructed everyone to turn off their torches, worried the mercenaries might spot them from below. Moving stealthily, Kabir glanced at the approach road to the Udaygiri caves. He could see a pair of bright headlights moving swiftly towards the hills.

"It's almost time," Kabir said as he pointed them out to the others. "Let's just keep moving quickly. They are still a few minutes away, we should reach the Jeep before they get here," he said, breaking into a run with the others following.

Anand, sitting in the driver's seat, spotted the silhouettes against the faint light of the moon moving quickly towards him. Trained to sense urgency, he manoeuvred the vehicle to pick them up as they neared him.

"Is there any other way out of here that does not use the road we came from?" Kabir asked the guard as he returned the keys and alerted him about the approaching mercenaries.

"But we need to go to the Heliodorus pillar first," Reeya interrupted him. She was by now confident of Kabir's abilities to get past the guards, even if it was after visiting hours.

Kabir nodded contritely as he realised he should have discussed the possible scenarios with Reeya before making any plans. He made a mental note to do so in future.

Anand suggested it would be prudent to first move away from there and then work out how best to get to the Heliodorus pillar. He turned off his headlights and pulled into the narrow street before the mercenaries had a chance to see them coming out from the cave complex. He was hoping that even if someone did turn onto the street, the distance and the darkness would provide them safe cover to escape.

"This road leads us straight to the Sanchi Stupa. We can then turn left and get back on the highway to circle back to the pillar," Reeya suggested.

Driving by moonlight, they were soon approaching the Stupa. Reeya was tempted to tell the others of its history and exquisite carvings, but decided it wasn't an opportune time.

Now at a safe distance, the driver turned on the headlights. The road veered left, and soon they approached the left turn on the highway to head to the Heliodorus Pillar. They were stunned to see the stationary taillights of the cars, trucks and buses in the traffic. The traffic was not moving at all for as far as Kabir's eyes could see.

"This does not look like a normal traffic jam," Kabir said softly. His gut feeling was that Myra was somehow responsible, though he had no way of knowing. They checked the maps to find that there were no other routes to the pillar.

"Do you have any suggestions?" he asked Reeya. "Should we spend the night somewhere nearby and start for the pillar at first light tomorrow morning?"

"Let's go to the *stupa* and find a place to rest." The historian in Reeya jumped at the opportunity. "There are no hotels or *dharmshalas* nearby that I know of. Maybe we can use the time to decipher any clues the cave has to offer while the images are still fresh in our minds."

The *stupa* was located in a large compound nearby, and Kabir was confident that the guards would let them in. He also saw it as a safe option as it was unlikely that anyone would expect them to be staying back. The thought of letting Myra and the mercenaries chase them unchecked bothered him, but this was the only way he could keep them close and find out what they knew. He didn't feel alarmed enough to ask for reinforcements, and besides, he preferred the radio silence, in case their intuition of a mole was right.

8

Sanchi Stupa

Day 1 | 2100 hrs

REEYA'S DAY HAD STARTED WITH SEEING THE DEAD BODY OF THE professor she had deeply admired. She had been chased all day by mercenaries capable of committing murders. Yet the anticipation of seeing the *stupa* pushed her emotional and physical fatigue into the background.

"I had first seen it as a child," she recalled. "I think it had a deep impact on me; it made me want to understand the mysteries of our civilisation."

The uniformed driver and Kabir's identity card got the group past the guards at the entry and allowed them to park the jeep in the designated area. Being a large compound, there was still some distance to be covered on foot. In her excitement, Reeya caught hold of Kabir's hand and led him to the entry gateway of the *stupa*. It was well-lit and could be seen clearly at night. Kabir could feel the spark as her fingers wrapped around his palm, but he knew she just wanted to share her excitement at seeing the monument again.

"See here," she pointed at the gateway that had all kinds of figures and motifs carved on it. "All the carvings here tell a story. There are stories and commentaries on the society right from the time of the Buddha's birth to major events in his life, up until these carvings were made.

"The original *stupa* was built around the third century BCE,[71] and the carvings and railings were added later. Most of them are from the second and first century BCE,"[72] Reeya said, pointing to the rich detail on the main gateway and the exquisitely crafted balustrades.

Although there was no mention of the *stupa* in the professor's clues, Kabir was glad of the distraction. His mind was still trying to work out if the mercenaries would follow them to the *stupa*. There was no way for them to know what clues were on the bracelet they had taken from the professor, but he felt confident that the *stupa* was not one of them. He wondered if the bracelet had any other clues that were not already known to them.

Besides, he reasoned, staying put would be a good option as they needed to head to the Heliodorus pillar anyway, before they could potentially solve the puzzle. Most likely, the mercenaries would assume that Kabir and Reeya were on their way to the airport. He felt relieved at the thought. The presence of the two *jawans* was also reassuring.

"What are these carvings here?" Kabir asked, pointing to the gateway that guarded the entry to the circumambulatory path around the *stupa*.

"That gateway is called a *Torana*. This one here is the Northern *Torana*, and it happens to be my favourite. When

I visited here as a child, I saw these *yakshini* figures as the protectors of the *stupa*[73] and all that it represented. I was just so excited to imagine that women had been given such a prominent role in this *Torana*. Of course, we continue to debate the role of *yakshinis* in ancient literature. They appear in many forms, from happily dancing spirits to haunting and punishing ones.[74] As a young girl, I was very inspired by their portrayal as strong and capable women," Reeya said, her eyes shining with admiration.

Kabir looked at the voluptuous female figures comfortably perched on a carved tree branch. Three of them seemed to be looking into the distance, ready to sound the alarm and go into battle. One looked towards the *stupa*, perhaps to symbolise that dangers could lurk within as well. The warning from Nair crossed his mind again: "Trust no one."

Reeya pointed to a panel that had figures dressed differently from the others. "These are Greeks, as evident from their typical attire of tunics, capes and sandals. We know Greece was a significant trading partner at the time, so there are cross-cultural influences between India and Greece in ancient times. And, if you're wondering about the Romans, they did not become an empire till much later."

As Kabir listened to Reeya, his overstretched imagination started to seek a connection between the Greek influence in the *stupa*[75] to the Heliodorus Pillar. *Were Myra and her team Greek?* he wondered. Realising that he was making too many connections between the dots, he dismissed the thought.

"There are many stories attached to these carvings. Let me show you another one that I like," Reeya continued enthusiastically as she walked clockwise towards the Eastern *Torana*.

Observing the vast amounts of intricate carvings that adorned the *stupa*, Kabir wondered—*This must have taken a large colony of skilled artisans to execute. I wonder where they disappeared?* He made a mental note to ask Reeya later.

They completed a quarter circle around the *stupa* and stood before the Eastern *Torana*. "This one here is interesting," Reeya said. "See how men and women are depicted as equals?" Reeya was looking up at the panels spanning the stone column.

"Each of these animal pairs is being ridden by a man and a woman—from rams to a camel and even a lion.[76] I always found these figures fascinating. I imagined them to be warriors and the guardians of the *stupa*. Of course, the stories these panels are based on are told in far greater detail in the Buddhist literature of the period," Reeya said with a smile. "But I prefer to believe that I have the freedom to interpret the carvings as I'd like, and not be tied to others' interpretations.

"Look at that carving." Reeya pointed to another stone panel that showed a woman sleeping on a bed supported by rails that looked like a miniature version of the Sanchi Stupa parapet. There was an elephant arriving at her feet from the skies above.

"This is Maya, the Buddha's mother. This panel tells us of a dream in which an elephant appeared and blessed her with a child.[77] As far as I know, this is one of the first instances of an immaculate conception recorded anywhere," Reeya said, turning to Kabir with a twinkle in her eyes.

Looking at Kabir's shocked expression, she continued, "It's interesting how things can be perceived differently when not seen from a Eurocentric point of view. Immaculate conceptions have been described in many cultures, before and after this one. But it is most widely associated with the birth of Jesus, given the cultural dominance of Christianity.

"Come, let me show you the southern one," Reeya said as she walked ahead, beckoning Kabir to follow. Kabir was still awestruck by the intricate details carved on the pillars. They wove a story for those who wanted to hear the stones speak.

Figure 4: *Main Gateway to the ancient city of Kusinagra in Magadha*

Image credit: Artist reconstruction of the Main Gateway to the ancient city of Kusinagara (cir. B.C. 500) in Magadha (Bihar). Adapted from a bas-relief on the Southern Gateway of the Great Stupa at Sanchi, Bhopal. Aided by image in "Indian Architecture (Buddha and Hindu Period" by Percy Brown, Published by D.B. Taraporevala and Sons, Pvt. Ltd. in Mumbai 1959. Public domain per Copyright Act of 1911"

Reaching the Southern *Torana*, Reeya first took a moment to go over it again herself, "It was the oldest and most intricately carved of the four *Toranas*.[78] Unfortunately, some of the carvings had been lost, but what remained was still exquisite. It was installed around the first or second century BCE during the time of the Sunga Dynasty."[79]

Pointing to the top of the *Torana*, she explained to Kabir. "See the carvings on that architrave? See how the city is under siege and the upper floors are filled with defenders?[80] Do you see the multi-storeyed edifices?"

Kabir tried to imagine what the city would have looked like. Reeya explained that these were the buildings of Kushinagara as it stood around 500 BCE.[81] Buddhists believe that it is the place where the Buddha left his body for the next world.

Kabir was looking up at the depiction of a city full of tall buildings that must have formed a beautiful skyline. He did not think that this level of urbanisation could have existed more than 2500 years ago.

"Look at the capital with the four lions facing in the four directions.[82] We use it today as our national emblem." Finally, something Kabir already knew about, and he smiled back at Reeya in acknowledgement.

"Lions were used extensively as a cultural motif. The one on the eastern pillar looks a lot like the Chinese or Singaporean depiction of the lion.[83] There was a lot of cross-cultural exchange in those days, though it is not always easy to trace the exact route.

"This will be more apparent on the Western *Torana*," Reeya said, approaching the next doorway to the *stupa*. "You may find similarities between the potbellied *Yakshas* carved on the capital and the Buddha depicted in other cultures. The various expressions of the *Yakshas* may also have been similarly interpreted by other cultures, resulting in the Laughing Buddha, the Sad Buddha, and so on. Of course, there are differing opinions, but the resemblance is uncanny," Reeya summed up.

Figure 5: *Western Torana at the Shanti Stupa*

Heading back to the Northern *Torana*, Kabir felt he had learned more from Reeya in one day than he had in many years of schooling.

"I only recall that we were made to memorise the dates of battles and the reigns of kings. We even did a few field trips, but I don't recall having learned about many such marvels, and more importantly, what they mean to us in the context of the timeline. Kabir said, adding with a thoughtful smile, "I like the way you explain."

Reeya thought to herself that he really ought to have paid more attention in class, but just smiled back.

They could hear a thunderstorm building up with lightning sporadically illuminating the inky black sky. The moon hid behind the clouds. The floodlights that had been illuminating the *stupa* were now turned off, as it was now 10 pm, leaving the campus dark except for a few lights illuminating the pathways. Moments later, it started raining heavily. Reeya and Kabir knew they would be soaking wet in seconds as the *Torana* was not going to shelter them. They rushed towards the nearest shelter, an ancient temple now known only as Temple 17[84], right next to the *stupa*.

In the few meters that they ran, they were already completely drenched. Water was running down their hair and faces, and their clothes were soaked. They carefully hurried up the temple steps, as the stone surface could be slippery. Standing in the verandah, safe from the rain, they watched it fall between the columns. The sight of the *stupa* getting illuminated from time to time by the lightning as the rain pelted down ferociously on it was wondrous.

"It looks like the rain may go on for a while," Kabir stated.

As the wind picked up, the rain started blowing into the verandah, forcing Reeya and Kabir to retreat further inside, into the temple chamber itself. At some point in history, the chamber may have had allure, but now, it was a bare shell. It was sound enough to provide them with shelter, though.

Feeling tired, Reeya went and sat in a corner. The downpour had intensified. Kabir realised that even if they could get to the Jeep, it was not likely that they could make it to the Heliodorus pillar. The rain was sure to have defeated any attempts to clear the traffic. It was better to just stay put. Kabir was sure Anand and Pratap would be on the watch for Myra and her crew.

Even though he understood that they lacked any better options, Kabir still paced the floor in his restlessness and anxiety to get moving. Eventually, even he felt tired and sat opposite Reeya on the floor. The silence felt uncomfortable, so he decided to broach the topic of the *stupa*.

Pointing to the uniformly cut and polished stone of the balustrade encircling the stupa, Kabir asked. "How do you think they made that? It is so even and precise, it almost seems to be made of concrete set with the help of moulds."

"Isn't it amazing that this was done in the second century BCE?" Reeya said ardently. "I find it amusing that we routinely see posts on social media that attribute all this magnificent building to aliens rather than our ancestors being advanced enough to use iron implements," her voice trailed off with a sigh.

"The ancient iron-producing civilisations that we have recently carbon-dated dot the map of India, Pakistan, all the way up to Afghanistan. The oldest use of iron seems to be in modern-day Tamil Nadu, dating back to 1200 BCE.[85] That's almost 3200 years ago! And of course, there was a steady stream of improved alloys also being made. Not to mention the six-ton iron pillar was created and installed right here, which still hasn't rusted.

"This balustrade tells me that the art of making high-quality iron had been perfected in this region by the time it was built and that, or a strong alloy such as steel, would have been used to make tools. These tools would have assisted in creating such uniform shapes and sizes, including the curvature of each stone in that railing. Today, we are open to seeing Indian history more objectively, and I am sure we will find a lot more innovative technology that was being used on a large scale," she concluded.

Almost as if on cue, Kabir's thoughts went right back to the question at hand. "Do you think any of these technologies were so revolutionary and valuable that people could commit murder to get their hands on them?"

Reeya was unable to think of anything that could merit such drastic actions on the part of some international syndicate. And yet, there was obviously something that had led to such a determined pursuit by those employing the mercenaries.

"I can't think of anything that we know of. Yet, the professor was obviously working on something that he felt would revolutionise the world." Reeya thought for a few moments and continued. "Also, the way the retort was kept in the cave, and its etchings, don't seem recent. It seems to have been left there for safekeeping several centuries ago."

Kabir tried to figure out what Reeya was saying. It stood to reason that the retort had remained hidden for several centuries. There may have been individuals or groups engaged in protecting certain secrets which could be dangerous if revealed. And yet, they did not destroy them, but only shielded them to be discovered at the right time in the future. Maybe now was the right time? He couldn't think of anything that would warrant someone going to such lengths as to hide and encode a message which they still had to decipher.

"Were you able to make sense of that message we saw on the retort?" Kabir enquired.

Reeya's mind was preoccupied with thoughts of who might have hidden the retort. Maybe if she could figure out the who and the when, the message would be easier to decode.

"No, but I am hoping that once we are at the Heliodorus column, something will click, and it will help me understand the message. I am also trying to think who may have hidden it," she said.

Kabir tried to make light of things in view of their grim situation, and said jokingly, "Oooh… it sounds like a secret cult to me."

Given the way the day had gone so far, she had not excluded such a possibility. "Many secret cults have been mentioned over the course of history. We have this romantic notion that they existed to protect the order of society or some advanced technology. Most of it is a myth. And even if such cults existed, they were to grab power for a select group. Few, if any, have existed to better the life of the common man. Honestly, I'd be even more worried if there were secret cults involved here."

Even as she said this, she felt a shiver run down her spine. The image of the *Yakshinis* flashed into her mind, and she thought, perhaps, it was an omen to help her channelise her strengths.

Reeya was starting to feel hungry and weak. They had not eaten since the tiffin in the jeep. As the torrential rain continued outside, she told Kabir that she was going to catch a nap.

Kabir could've done with some shut-eye, too, but he decided to stand guard. "You go ahead. We need your mind to be fresh and alert. I'll wake you up when we are ready to move."

He watched the rain pour over the remains of the Ashoka pillar standing next to the *stupa*. Seeing the edicts inscribed on it in an ancient language, he made a mental note to ask Reeya what the language was and what the edicts said. He also thought about how different the day had been for him. For the first time in months, he had not been tormented by the loss of Vani. He realised he was enjoying Reeya's company.

The rain had just about stopped, and Kabir could see the first signs of dawn on the horizon. He decided it was time to walk up to the jeep and see how they were doing. He went back towards the entrance, where they had parked, but there was no jeep in sight.

9

Heliodorus Pillar

Day 2 | 0600 hrs

KABIR'S FIRST THOUGHT WAS TO IMAGINE THE WORST—A TRAIT that had helped him stay alive more than once. Had the mercenaries got them, and were they now surrounding the Stupa to capture Kabir and Reeya? He was about to dart back to Reeya when he saw a vehicle approaching. He recognised their jeep and breathed a sigh of relief.

Turned out, they had stepped away momentarily to bring them all some bread *pakoda*, a *dhaba* classic. The breakfast was accompanied by tomato ketchup and hot *masala chai* in earthen pots.

Kabir asked anyway, "Where did you guys go?" his tone indicated displeasure at their having abandoned the post. Kabir knew fully well that they did not see this as a wartime assignment, but he wanted to impress on them the gravity of the situation.

"There is a *dhaba* around the corner, *saab*. We left the jeep parked hidden away at the edge and walked to the *dhaba*. I'm sure no one recognised us as on-duty *jawans*. And we did not see anyone suspicious. We also made some discrete inquiries. But nothing. No one has been asking any questions," said Pratap as he handed over the food package to Kabir.

Kabir thanked him and proceeded back to the temple, where he was expecting to find Reeya still asleep. But she was in the front of the temple, awake and seated between the pillars.

"Looks like a beautiful morning," Kabir remarked, handing the breakfast to Reeya. "Did you get some sleep?"

"Yes, I was so tired," Reeya replied, thankful for a few hours of rest.

Opening the package, she handed Kabir a delicious-looking bread *pakoda*.

Kabir took his bread *pakoda* and proceeded to eat quickly. "We need to get out of here quickly," he said thickly in between bites.

Kabir took the crumpled food packaging and threw it into a trash can on their way back to the jeep. "If we all threw our garbage in the proper place, there would be nothing left to be cleaned up," Kabir said importantly as if imparting a lesson in civic sense.

It did make sense in the context of a country where the vast majority did not make that extra effort, or there aren't enough, conveniently placed, trash cans. "At least we have tidied up after ourselves and left the *stupa* site clean," Reeya said, smiling encouragingly at him.

Soon, they were on their way to the Greek column. It was still very early in the morning, and the sun hadn't had time to dry up the puddles left by the rain. The dampness in the air and the lush, green trees made it feel like they were driving through a tropical forest.

As they reached the highway, they saw the overturned truck that had blocked the traffic the night before. The local municipality workers had managed to pull it to one side to allow for traffic to pass through slowly, but had not yet managed to turn it the right side up to tow it away.

As they drove past it, Kabir sensed that the angle it was lying pointed to a deliberate overturning. His gut feeling returned. He was almost certain Myra had something to do with this to prevent him and Reeya from getting out of the Udaygiri caves.

They drove straight to the pillar. After the magnificence of the stupa, Kabir found the pillar unimpressive. Reeya explained that it was not built there but given as a gift by the Greek Ambassador Heliodorus to the local Sunga king in the second century BCE.[86] It was found to be held in place by iron wedges driven perpendicularly into the ground.[87]

Situated in a large community park with a shoulder-high gated fence, the pillar was easily accessible with only a low platform around it. Amusingly, the locals had given the pillar a demi-god status, and often gathered around to pray to it, calling it *Khamba Baba*, or the Pillar Sage.

Reeya was not interested in talking about its history and just wanted to get close to it to examine it. Approaching the gate, she struggled to open it until the jammed latch gave way. The surface of the pillar was covered in neat rows and columns of writing in an ancient script. Reeya instantly recognised it as Brahmi script—one of the most ancient scripts to have been deciphered and the precursor to most scripts in and around India.[88]

Reeya touched the pillar lightly, as if feeling its history and inviting it to tell her what mystery it was guarding. She reached into her bag and took the retort out. With her gaze fixated on the retort, she tried to make sense once more of what the etchings could have meant.

Reeya compared the pillar etched on the retort with the one that stood before her and was sure it was the same. She looked at the short and long lines and then looked up at the nine neatly engraved lines of script on the pillar.

"What if these codes tell us what characters to pick from the pillar, based on the row and column?" Reeya shared her thoughts out loud with Kabir.

"It could be. Perhaps, the vertical lines just separate the column and row position, each set being an ordered pair?" Kabir said, building on her speculation. "But how would the short and long dashes give us a number?"

The question triggered a thought in Reeya's head. "Of course, it would make perfect sense if these were binary numbers. Just as we write zeros and ones today, the original binary was formed using light and heavy 'syllables' by Rishi Pingala."[89]

"Who is Rishi Pingala, and why was he experimenting with binary?" Kabir was not sure he understood. "More importantly, can you decode this?"

"I guess we will soon find out," said Reeya with a confident smile that reassured Kabir. Reeya had a hypothesis on how to decode the symbols on the retort. "Indian civilisation has had exposure to the place value system, including binary and decimal, for a very long time. You do know that the first recorded use of the decimal place value system was here, right?"

"You mean Arabic numerals?" Kabir was not quite sure what she meant. He knew that Arabic numerals were not of Arabic origin. They were given that name by European traders transacting with Arab merchants who made use of these numerals. And in a Eurocentric knowledge system, that name stuck.

"Numerals are one thing, and yes, they were of Indian origin. I don't think anyone disputes that. The 'decimal place value' is the basis of common math today. It's how you would write, say, 20+7 as 27. Starting from the right, each digit has a place value based on a power of 10. Each place will represent 1s, 10s, 100s, 1000s and so on. These were likely extensively used in ancient India, and examples can be seen even in the *Vedas* from the second to the first century BCE,"[90] Reeya explained.

"I knew that our ancient civilisation invented the zero, but never realised that there was more to it. And by the looks of it—a lot more!" Kabir was getting a sense of the expanse of the subject.

Reeya smiled and decided to spare Kabir a detailed lecture on the subject. It has been argued that Rishi Panini's metalinguistic grammar rules, dating to the mid-fifth century BCE,[91] stimulated the early development of algebra and the number system in India. She focused on the task of solving the binary code, as she continued explaining.

"Rishi Pingala is known more for other things rather than for his contribution to the binary system. He explicitly referred to the word '*shunya*', which later became the standard mathematical term for 'zero'.[92] He lived in the third or second century BCE and is also known to have documented what later became the Fibonacci Series.[93] He constructed the *Maathra-meru* mountain, now called the Pascal triangle,[94] almost a thousand years before Pascal or Fibonacci were even born," Reeya said while continuing to examine the codes to see if they fit the pattern. Kabir just stared at Reeya in admiration.

"The first part of the code reads '--- --- | --- - ---', which would be 11|101 in binary. That is 3|5 as in our normal decimal numbers. Similarly, these others would then read 3|6 and 7|6 respectively," Reeya said, doing a quick binary conversion.

Kabir was already looking up the third row and moving his finger to the fifth letter in the third row on the 2200-year-old column.

"Here, this one," Kabir pointed it out to Reeya. "Do you think you can read these?"

Kabir wondered if he sounded insensitive, doubting her ability, but she moved her eyes to where he was pointing, "Sure. It's classic Brahmi script."

She continued to assemble the characters based on the sequence etched on the earthen retort. Writing them on a piece of paper, she looked at them.

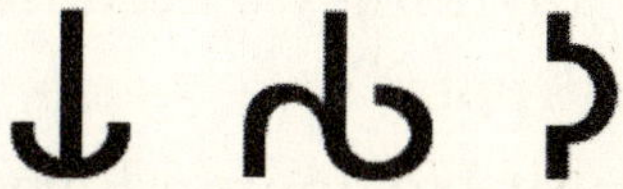

Figure 6: *"Ya Sa Da" in Brahmi Script*

"It spells '*Yasada*', which is interesting." Kabir waited for Reeya to continue. "It makes sense. *Yasada* means zinc.[95] The ancients were well-versed in extracting zinc, as it was used in making brass.[96] I can now say with certainty that there is spent zinc ore inside this retort, and it was at some point used to distil zinc, most likely where much of it was distilled during that time, in a town called Zawar[97]."

They both looked at each other, in some ways feeling satisfied that they had managed to solve a puzzle left by the ancients. But it did not help them figure out how it was connected to the professor's murder and what it was that the mercenaries were after.

"So where do we go from here?" inquired Kabir, fully aware that Reeya would want to make Zawar the next stop.

Reeya was now holding up the zinc-ore-holding retort and turning it around to examine the carvings. "Why hide just this one retort in Udaygiri as a clue pointing to Zawar?"

Reeya assumed that Zawar held the key to the next link in the chain. But she did have a point, which now became more important. *Who would have left this trail of breadcrumbs and why?*

"Where is Zawar anyway? I have never heard of it," Kabir asked, once again looking to Reeya for answers. "But more importantly, is there anything we need from here? Or should we head back to the airport?"

"Zawar is a town near Udaipur in Rajasthan. I am not sure where we will find answers in Zawar, but I doubt we will find anything else here," Reeya said as she took some pictures of the column for later reference.

Paradoxically, Kabir had felt better when he knew the mercenaries were on his tail. He could predict their moves and knew what to expect of them. But with no sign of them, he was starting to feel uneasy.

Reeya was excited about having figured out the puzzle that was now taking them to Zawar, but something was still nagging her. As they got into the jeep to go to the airport, Reeya was wondering about the use of the word for zinc—*yasada*. Though zinc had been extracted since the third century BCE or even earlier,[98] it wasn't until the 13th century CE that the word *yasada* was used for it.[99]

Why the time lag? All other clues have been from very ancient times. Reeya could not find an explanation for the discrepancy in the timeline. *Unless there were others nearly eight centuries ago who wanted to keep something a secret. A secret the professor unearthed but didn't want disclosed to the wrong people.*

She realised this cat-and-mouse game had been played before. The thought that it was an 800-year-old mystery that had led to murder sent a shiver down her spine.

10
Skyros

A GLEAMING WHITE 2000-TON SUPER YACHT FLOATED weightlessly on the clear water of a cove near an island in the Aegean Sea. Beautiful bikini-clad women lounged on the front deck, soaking in the sun through a thick layer of suntan lotion. A deep blue tropical drink sat at an arm's length.

Inside the glass chamber, the temperature was much more comfortable than the humid, exquisitely warm outdoors. A large balding man sat on a leather couch, facing several screens that monitored every heartbeat of his business transactions. There was a trace of his Greek heritage in his looks, but it was unmistakable in his accent as he spoke to his wife.

"You should just leave me alone to run my business. It was a big mistake to bring you here," the irritation in his voice was apparent.

Nearby, Themis—his wife of thirty years, and the person largely responsible for building the business that the Greek thought of as his own—smirked. She continued to nurse her scotch in a large whisky glass with a single cube of ice.

"Ezio, you are going to pop a vein one of these days. You just don't listen. You need to drop this stupid quest while you still can."

Themis, now at an age where the wrinkles showed as a graceful manifestation of wisdom, walked closer to Ezio. Perhaps she was hoping he would take his gaze away from the monitors and actually look at her. Standing next to his console, she continued in her exasperated yet loving tone, like a mother chiding her child.

"Ezio, people have already died in this quest. You are delusional to think you are the rightful heir of what could be a mythical object." Themis had been against this quest from the start and was now getting nervous seeing Ezio so obsessed.

It had not always been like this. Ezio had been a promising young man when they had met and fallen in love. His fascination with the ancient had made him a name in the high society that Themis belonged to. Together, along with Themis's father's small fortune, the couple had done well for themselves. Ezio's passion for antiques and Themis' connections opened doors to many celebrities. With time and trust, many knocked at his door for his ability to manage a questionable shipment.

Leveraging the continued expansion, he also set up new distribution channels for drugs, arms, ammunition, and even human trafficking. He was now the king of shipping routes that moved cargo and contraband alike.

Themis had played an active role in managing the relationships with the who's who as Ezio had expanded his dark empire. She looked past the suntan-lotion-covered playthings that Ezio enjoyed keeping on the yacht. She thought of them as harmless entertainment. But this was different. Now it was no longer about pleasure or money. It had all started one day when he returned from his 'ceremony'.

Ezio had often visited the Church located on an atoll not far from the eastern tip of the Skyros island in the Aegean Sea. It was a desolate spot, away from civilisation. The single-chamber church had been renovated at the turn of the last century, but had stood there for much longer. For those who enjoyed a good dive in clear blue waters, this place was heaven. But the last visit was different. This time, there was a passenger who would come back with him from the nearby island of Eresos.

Eresos was a beautiful Greek Island where time seemed to have stood still, dotted as it was with rustic eateries and small curio shops. It was also home to many Orthodox churches frequented by families over many generations. It was rumoured that Alexander the Great had cast two loyalists on this island as traitors so that they could unearth plans of any possible revolt.

The group of traitors comprised traders, artisans, courtesans, and the diplomat and historian, Megasthenes. Megasthenes wrote a work that became the lens through which the European world viewed the mysterious land, far from Greece, that Alexander never ruled. Called *Indica*, it was a definitive collection of the ordinary, embellished with the mystical. No copy of the four-volume work had ever been found, though portions of it had been reconstructed through references in other works.

Ezio had received a message that he had to pick up this special passenger from Eresos and to take him along to the night ceremony in the church of Saint Ermolaos, on the eastern tip of Skyros.

Ezio was familiar with the esoteric ceremony, which served as a renewal of vows of secrecy and sharing of information. It had helped Ezio in his life of chasing art and crime alike. The request to bring someone was unusual, but something he could easily comply with.

The passenger, dressed as a priest, did not say much as he boarded from Eresos. Despite no words being exchanged, Ezio sensed an air of authority which only comes with a lifetime of being revered or feared. The priest somehow reminded him of a Jedi, as though he possessed certain supernatural powers. He carried with him an assortment of artefacts from an elaborately embellished stone-studded Greek cross to an unimpressive string of carved wooden beads. He also carried what seemed like a book wrapped in a red cotton cloth.

The priest was accorded the reverence and the liberty that his aura demanded. Not many words were exchanged, and Ezio felt that was how the priest wanted it.

Ezio was dressed as he always was for these rituals: hand-spun cotton threaded sparingly with gold. Select pieces of jewellery and sandals completed his ensemble. The passenger seemed uncomfortable in his hooded habit made of thick grey fabric, but he did not complain.

Ezio moored his yacht away from the little atoll and lowered the small wooden dinghy to take them to the island for the night of the ceremony.

They entered the small, renovated church and proceeded towards the confessionals. Ezio knew his way around and found the hidden stairs to the basement. Both men descended the steps leading to a spacious basement that would be hard to imagine on the small atoll.

The high, ornate ceilings were covered with what was once a magnificent fresco. It had faded with time but still gleamed richly in the light of the hundreds of candles that lit the room. Intricate iconography adorned the walls as well. The marble floor was laid out in the shape of the star of David. Each segment was in a different marble, ostensibly brought from a different location.

A red marble encircled the star with embedded circular brass plates placed about six inches apart. Each of the brass plates served as a candle holder. The lit candles imparted a golden hue to the congregation that was gathered around for the ritual, chanting and gesturing as if in a trance.

Ezio joined the ongoing ceremony without a word. The priest continued to walk past the ceremony and disappeared behind a set of heavy, black velvet curtains.

The elaborate ceremony continued uninterrupted, with the various participants, well-versed in the rituals, performing them effortlessly.

At the appropriate moment of transition in the rituals, a man dressed in white robes walked behind Ezio and summoned him with a gentle tap on the shoulder. Ezio got up and followed him to the chamber that lay behind the black velvet curtains.

The elders were assembled around a semi-circular table. Each had a heap of trinkets that must have symbolised something to them. The man in a white robe gestured to Ezio to sit on a bare wooden stool that faced the elders. He had dreamed of this day since he had heard of this ceremony.

At the appropriate time in the ritual, the leader of the ceremony asked Ezio to enter an alcove where the priest sat waiting for him.

Each of the elders got up one at a time as they chanted and sprinkled him with water from a round, ornate, antique copper vessel.

Once they all had their turn, they handed him a box that was wrapped in a red cotton cloth. Ezio had seen the red cloth used for wrapping ancient artefacts earlier. He knew it was ancient Indian cotton dyed in the red colour obtained from processing the root of a *Majeeth* plant.[100]

"Much blood has been spilt to find this and keep it safe," the priest spoke in a deep, authoritative voice that reverberated in the chamber. He carefully proceeded to unwrap the box and place it on the table before him. A single fighter mounted on a horse next to what seemed like a stream of water, a river perhaps, was carved on the lid. The brass hinges and the clasp that kept it shut showed their age but looked highly functional.

With a gentle click to undo the clasp, the priest proceeded to open it. The hinges worked smoothly, and the box opened without the creaks that should have been heard due to its age.

The inside of the wooden box was polished to a gloss. A well-folded red cloth shaped like an envelope protected the contents that sat in the compartment. The lid fit so perfectly that not even a speck of dust had entered it over the centuries.

Ezio reverentially picked up the red cloth parcel and proceeded to gingerly unwrap it to see the contents. A series of well-aged palm leaves had letters beautifully painted in black Indian ink. The script was an ancient variant of Greek. As Ezio held the pages in his hand, trying to read them, the priest put his hand on Ezio's shoulder.

"These pages you hold are believed to have been written along with the *Indica*. Read them carefully. They describe a cauldron that the brotherhood has shed much blood in trying to obtain. You have been chosen to bring it back to us. It is your destiny now. You must not fail."

The priest's remarks were cryptic. Ezio was still confused as to why it involved him personally. "Spend time to imbibe the words and you will understand."

The ceremony concluded at dawn, with the participants entering the water fully clothed to worship the rising Sun.

Ezio studied the manuscript that described a cauldron that seemed to have a bizarre power. The more he studied the manuscript, the more he understood why this was going to be important to him personally. His research now led him to understand the possible power described and, perhaps more significantly for Ezio, a potential ancestral connection as well.

Ever since that day, Ezio had been obsessed with finding the clues that would lead him to the cauldron. He fervently believed in what was written on the pages inked more than two millennia ago. He had used his extensive empire to find every piece of information that he could to complete the puzzle.

He understood that finding the cauldron would significantly enhance his business, and also convinced himself that it was his sacred obligation. Themis had seen her husband becoming obsessed and neglecting the business. She had stepped in to soothe the irate associates who had not been able to reach Ezio for their business. "Ezio, stop this mindless pursuit," she had advised her husband, but it only irritated him further.

Novak had been loyal to Ezio and had stepped up to help Themis run the business. It was his chance to show his worth and rise. Themis had a good grip of the business, but she needed Ezio to do his part, especially on the shady side of it. She needed his obsession to end before it was too late.

Themis was in her room late one evening when Novak brought in some papers. "Themis, I need you to review and approve these shipments. I am not able to find Ezio, and these are urgent, or else the shipments will be held up. Pablo will not be happy," Novak had said.

Themis had always liked his sense of humour. He knew the client wasn't Pablo, but he was alluding to a Latin client who somehow seemed the incarnation of the famous drug lord.

"Leave it here, I'll sign it. First, I need your help in removing the kink in my back," Themis had said, removing her robe as she lay on her back. Novak was expecting it, but the sight of her naked back made him uncomfortable and scared. If Ezio saw him touch her, he would have had his head.

The hesitation was obvious to Themis, so when Novak mustered the courage to say that he would be right back with the masseuse, she was far from disappointed and had a smirk on her face. Leaving the stack of papers and other belongings on the desk, Novak excused himself. That was when Themis decided she needed to find a way to help Ezio in his search.

Quickly, she brought out the ornate box that was well guarded in the safe in her room. Carefully exposing the palm leaves to the camera in the smartphone that Novak had left behind, she scanned her mental list of who would be in the best position to help. She had established good relationships with dealers and connoisseurs of antiquities over the years of being in the business. She had pondered on how best to stop Ezio and decided that Professor Ghosh would be a good choice. He was known for his integrity and tenacity. She believed he would be able to complete Ezio's quest, allowing Ezio to focus on the business and her again. It would be days before the full effect of her actions would be apparent to her or anyone else. And certainly not in the way she had intended.

Damn the professor! Ezio thought to himself. *Why did he have to interfere?* The interference had not only cost the professor his life, but it had also caused a sizable setback in Ezio's plans. He was determined to get things back on track. He must have what he felt was rightfully his. *I must stop the professor's understudy from messing with my plans.*

He picked up his phone and dialled his contact. "You have had enough time to stop the two amateurs in your way. Take off the kid gloves and get rid of them. We need to do what we set out to do," Ezio said in an impatient tone.

"Ezio, you need to stop calling me," replied the deep voice on the other end of the phone. "It is a dangerous mission, and you are making it worse. Leave the amateurs to me."

The firm tone reminded Ezio that he was not in control of the action on the ground, which further infuriated him. "Fine, you have forty-eight hours. After that, I will take matters into my hands!"

It was time to instruct Myra to deal with Kabir and Reeya. They were not part of the equation, and even though it would be a waste of good talent, it had to be done.

11
Bhopal

Day 2 | 1000 hrs

THE JEEP QUICKLY MOVED TOWARDS THE BHOPAL AIRPORT.

As her eyes feasted on the sprawling fields, Reeya's mind went back to the whirlwind adventure that the last twenty-four hours had been. She forced her attention to the retort and the clues she had collected. Her brain was trying to conjure up the circumstances of the night that the professor was killed.

Kabir was thinking along the same lines and knew that only Reeya would be able to piece things together. "Any theories?" Kabir asked as he saw Reeya lost in thought.

From the corner of his eye, he noticed an SUV starting to creep up to their jeep and a window being rolled down. His keenly honed instincts made him see some movement in the depths of the SUV.

"Gun! Gun! Brake hard! Now!" yelled Kabir as he pulled Reeya down and threw his body over her to shield her from any incoming bullets.

The driver, a trained military operative, had also seen the SUV approach and responded instantly by braking hard. The jeep skid sideways on the wet road to the low embankment and ended up on the service road running alongside the highway. The bullet shattered the driver's window, barely missing him, and exited from the windshield, making a clean hole.

With the jeep now stopped on the service road, Kabir reached for his service gun as he got out and started to shoot. They could see the SUV slowing down, clearly intending to come back for them. But seeing Kabir and Pratap shooting at them, those in the SUV thought otherwise and sped away, merging with the traffic.

Kabir gestured urgently to the driver to follow the SUV. The army jeep was a spirited vehicle and clawed its way back up the embankment and onto the highway. But the SUV had put a lot of distance between them, and Kabir could not see it anymore.

"Speed up! We need to find them!" Kabir ordered as adrenaline snapped his senses into focus. His vision narrowed on the highway ahead, scanning for the disappearing SUV. His clenched fist made his veins stand out on his muscular forearm, tensed by frustration. *We cannot let them get away with this!* Kabir thought to himself. *But how did they know where to find and ambush us?*

"Can your radio catch the police band?" Kabir asked the *jawans* as he pointed to the contraption mounted on the dashboard.

"It is supposed to, but I have never done it. Let me try," Pratap tried to tune into the police channel. Kabir hoped to hear something about the SUV, but instead, what they heard made their heart sink.

"...repeat. Suspects are heading towards Bhopal on the Bhopal-Vidisha highway. One male and one female suspect have fired at and killed an army *jawan* and taken another hostage. They are also wanted in connection with a murder in Patna. Approach with caution." No one sitting in the jeep could believe that the tables had been turned on them.

The driver, having just dodged the bullet, was laughing. "It's not every day you hear about your death on the radio." He continued in a humorous tone, "It would seem obvious that you are being set up, sir. There is no one better qualified than me to answer that you did not shoot me."

"Anand, they may kill you just to prove their story. So don't take it lightly," Kabir cautioned.

What worried Kabir more was how the mercenaries had managed to put out a fake radio alert on the police channel. They had to be tech-savvy, but did they have someone helping them from the inside?

"Drop us near a busy area and head back to your base before someone takes another shot at you. You will be safe there, and you can explain what happened to your officer-in-charge." Kabir was now worried for their safety.

Kabir took his cell phone and broke it in half, and tossed it out of the window. "Yeah, I know I shouldn't litter," he said with a serious expression as he extended his hand, asking Reeya for her cell phone. She froze momentarily and calculated the damage that was going to be done, and then handed over her phone. "I think I have it backed up," she whispered.

Kabir proceeded to break and dispose of her phone as well. He then decided it was also too risky to use the coms device the deputy chief had given him and threw it out of the window. He kept the cash and the gun. The false identity cards were most likely also compromised, but he chose to keep those for now.

"I'll drop you off at the next village, which is just a few kilometres away. You'd be able to take a bus from there. Just be careful and keep a low profile," Anand suggested. He presumed there would be a lot of police looking for Kabir and Reeya.

The village was like many others in the area. There were a few shops selling the basics. A few *dhabas* clustered around a mechanic shop that mostly fixed tractors in the vicinity.

With luck, a bus would stop by, and Kabir was hoping they could both get on it. For a little while, he'd have to operate without the help of the deputy chief. As he started analysing everything that had happened recently, he was sure the mercenaries had tracked their cell phones. There was no other way Myra would have reached them.

A truck, carrying labourers in the back, stopped. Daily-wagers often hitch-hiked along the highway and were dropped off at nearby projects. Since they were paid only minimum wages, it was the only way the labourers could reach their work sites without walking all the way or draining the little they earned.

Obviously, Kabir and Reeya couldn't pass off as labourers, but it was probably the best way to get to civilisation.

Kabir was certain that a solution would emerge once they reached the nearest town. "I'm guessing we will not be taking a flight just yet," Reeya said, reading his mind. Kabir nodded and outlined his plan, "We should head to Bhopal. I'm sure we can find a way once there."

The drive was bumpy, and they were charged far more than the labourers would be paying. But Kabir was grateful for having found a ride at all. Kabir thanked the driver as he dropped them off on the outskirts of the city.

"We will continue on foot from here for a little while and later take an autorickshaw. I have a contact in the city. Hopefully, he can help us." Kabir told Reeya.

Kabir had cultivated and maintained an assortment of informants over the course of working in covert operations. It was time to bring some in. He instructed the autorickshaw driver where to go.

The ride through the town was chaotic, and the autorickshaws were a convenient size to navigate through narrow streets. Reeya insisted on taking a newer, electric one. They were just as nimble, minus the noise and the fumes of the two-stroke engine.

Yassir was the owner of a nightclub in a large shopping mall, located in the centre of town. A colourful and energetic man, Yassir was a micromanager. He considered himself meticulous and indispensable, and could often be heard yelling at his workers. He firmly believed that they needed to be treated like slaves, and if he did not instruct them loudly, nothing would get done.

As soon as Yassir saw Kabir and Reeya enter the establishment, he made for the back entrance as quickly as his rather bulky body allowed him to.

"Stop, and come back here, Yassir. You couldn't outrun a two-year-old, let alone me. And you know that," Kabir said loudly, with a laugh as if to mock Yassir into obeying.

Yassir realised the futility of it and stopped in his tracks. "What do you want from me this time?" complained Yassir as he slowly walked to Kabir. "You cost me my liquor licence the last time we encountered each other. You know how difficult it is to run a nightclub without a liquor licence? I cannot help you. We are even. Just go away," Yassir tried to dismiss Kabir, knowing full well that this time, too, Kabir would only bring bad luck.

"Yassir, Yassir, you should be thanking me that you still have this nice place here," chided Kabir. "Ah, the liquor licence. You do know that it had nothing to do with me, right? I did not bring the drugs you got caught with. Stop blaming me, or maybe this time we will find something even more interesting."

Kabir knew Yassir was resourceful and could be helpful with a little arm-twisting. He continued with a sly smile for encouragement, "Let's be honest, you do like to help me catch the bad guys, now, don't you?"

With a wary, resigned look on his face, Yassir said, "Tell me what you want and then get out of here. You are bad for business."

"Oh, Yassir. After all the care I take of you," joked Kabir, making Yassir squirm some more. "Just get me a safe transport out of here to Udaipur."

"You mean to say they won't send you a jet on demand? What did you do? Did they catch on to your shady dealings?" It was Yassir's turn to make fun of Kabir. "I hope they find you and burn you in hell! Why would I help you?"

Kabir gave him a stern look. Yassir knew he was in Kabir's debt for having saved his life more than once. The look told Yassir that Kabir was serious, and the posturing had to wait.

"You are in trouble, aren't you? Don't tell me. I don't want to know. I'll get into trouble too." Yassir took a step back but continued with the attitude. "I'll find a way to get you out. But it won't be comfortable, and it will cost you."

"Now!" Kabir said firmly.

"Ok. Ok. I got it. Now." Yassir could sense the urgency in Kabir's voice. Nevertheless, Yassir felt it was a good opportunity to have some fun at Kabir's expense. It was a small payback for the business he had lost the last time Kabir had visited.

Turning to Kabir and Reeya, he continued. "You are not going anywhere looking like this. Too easy to spot." Yassir said while scratching the back of his head and looking around. "I think you need to look like two working hands running away to get married. Ah, because you are from different castes and your families would not accept the wedding." He was starting to smirk as he conjured up the script.

"But you are in luck. Follow my man to the back room. There are some clothes you can change into." Yassir's smirk turned to a smile as he imagined Kabir in the gaudy wedding outfit. He also felt satisfied putting to good use the costumes left behind by the dance troupe that had performed the night before. Kabir tried to mask his feeling of horror with a forced smile as he sensed what he was about to be subjected to. Speaking with playful authority, he continued, "Don't complain and just change into those."

Before Kabir could say anything, Reeya chipped in, "Ok, we'll do it!"

She was enjoying the chase and found the idea of disguises pretty exciting. Seeing her child-like enthusiasm, Kabir mumbled that it was not a game.

"Pick a caste you want to be from. And at least pretend you want to marry me." She was now having fun with the role-playing and decided to pick what might pass for a cheap bridal outfit.

Having made sure that Kabir and Reeya looked their part, Yassir was now deriving some more entertainment. "Oh, and make sure you wear those shoes," he said, pointing to the old-fashioned leather *jutties*. Reeya was already accessorising her rather ornate *ghagra choli* outfit with bold multicoloured bangles. Kabir couldn't help but smile as Reeya pranced around in the borrowed wedding dress. Reeya's exaggerated attempt at walking in character almost made him laugh.

Kabir grudgingly thanked Yassir as the two left, following the errand boy to the warehouse. Reeya walked ahead of Kabir energetically, with a bounce in her feet. Following her, Kabir couldn't help but notice how the outfit was enhancing her curves. He felt drawn to her hair that moved with the bounce of her step over the backless blouse.

He forced his attention back, not without an involuntary smile, though, as he watched Reeya move sensuously towards the truck. Her bag, still carrying the artefacts picked up along the way, stood out like a sore thumb.

The truck was partially filled with large cardboard cartons. There was a distinct smell of liquor, but Kabir was not particularly interested in finding out if it was illicit. They got into the truck, and more boxes were loaded, hiding them from view.

It was quite suffocating once the loading door had been latched up. Kabir teased Reeya, "Did you also carry mosquito spray in that bag of yours? Do carry it next time."

Reeya acknowledged with a smile. She had grown rather fond of Kabir. She looked away as she blushed, thinking of the possibility of a next time.

Kabir was impressed by how easily Reeya was ready to do whatever was required. She hadn't made any fuss through the entire adventure. Having spent time with her, he had to acknowledge he was getting rather fond of her.

Dressed in ethnic garb, he decided to use the native tongue of the area. Imitating the local accent and using the familiar *tu* rather than the more refined *tum* or *aap* to address her, he asked Reeya if she was comfortable.

Reeya could see Kabir was trying to make light of the situation, and replied laughing, in a similar vein, "I'll be comfortable so long as I'm alive..." Pausing for the effect and to watch Kabir, she continued with an exaggerated smile. "And with you. Let's run away to another town where no one can find us." Kabir smiled with a confused look.

As the truck started to move, fresh air came in, making it less stuffy. It was still early evening, and they wouldn't reach Udaipur before dawn. They had nearly ten hours to kill. Thankfully, Yassir had given them some packed food for the long ride.

"I would have packed margaritas for you, but I really don't want more liquor on that truck!" Yassir laughed at his own joke, handing them the packed food.

"What will we find in Udaipur?" Kabir asked, deciding to turn the conversation towards the investigation.

Typically, Reeya took a moment to answer as she collected her thoughts. It was a trait that Kabir was getting used to when he asked a question of Reeya.

"It's not Udaipur that we will be going to. It's a nearby town called Zawar—it's is a mining town." Reeya paused and then decided to start from the beginning.

"Well, it's also not just Zawar. The entire stretch from Jaipur to beyond Zawar was a very fertile stretch of land that was also quite rich in minerals, and it saw many early civilisations. Many of these settlements were contemporary with the Harappans, forming the Indus Valley civilisation.

"Just to give you a context, while this stretch saw one of the earliest settlements, mining activity began much later. And we still continue to find older artefacts in the region that push the settlement dates further back. Zawar was one such village, and it was, most likely, the first to produce zinc, a key ingredient for making brass." Reeya paused to see Kabir listening intently and continued.

"Someday, I would love to see the open mines and multilayered shaft mining there. It is said that the people of Zawar came up with a very innovative technique for smelting zinc. And for more than a thousand years, they were the only ones who could separate zinc from its ore[101]. Do you realise what it means?" Reeya asked.

Kabir, though listening intently, did not know how to answer. "Do tell," he asked simply.

"It means that almost all the brass you see in the ancient world, including in Europe, is likely made of zinc extracted in Zawar![102]" Reeya exclaimed. Not sure Kabir was grasping the enormity of the industrial capability that Zawar represented, she added, "You know, don't you, that India accounted for over a quarter of the world's economy in ancient times? That would equate to the ancient Indian economy having a larger share of the world economy than the US does today. And Zawar was in part responsible for it."

Kabir hadn't known it, but awestruck with the comparison, he let out a whistle of surprise. "Wow! You mean to say that we had such a developed industrial output back then? And to think we only associate our ancient civilisation with religious mythology," Kabir said, sounding astounded by the fact.

"So where were the Greeks and the Romans back then?" Kabir asked, curious about other advanced civilisations he knew of.

"The Roman Empire came much later—circa 50 BCE,"[103] Reeya replied. "While Alexander was conquering Persia around 330 BCE,[104] zinc was already being produced in Zawar.[105] Though we don't yet have physical evidence of large-scale smelting until a later date, we will likely find it in the lower layers of those mountains." Reeya said, pointing to a series of hills nearby. "These are man-made hills, the result of centuries of spent zinc ore and the retorts piled up around the town.[106] And all this was heaped before other civilisations had figured out how to distil zinc from its ore.

"Even as recently as 1748, the world had not found a more efficient way of producing zinc. In fact, that year, William Champion tried to patent what resembled the Zawar method in Bristol, in the UK.[107] So you can imagine how advanced our industrial process was."

The back of the truck was not uncomfortable, largely due to the thick cotton cushions that Yassir had laid down, and as long as the truck was moving and fresh air kept coming in, Kabir was almost enjoying the slow road to Udaipur. He felt, what he was just getting to know from Reeya should have been taught in high school.

"So, what do we expect to find in Zawar?" The question was still on Kabir's mind.

"I don't know what we will find," Reeya's voice trailed off.

"The professor had once introduced me to the dean of the archaeology department of Poorvi Vidyapeeth, located in Udaipur. I am inclined to approach him and ask what this could mean. As fascinated as I am by the thought of seeing the ancient mines, I am scared of crawling into one to find more," Reeya shuddered.

Kabir wanted to probe more; he felt she had the answers they were looking for, even if she didn't know it yet. But seeing her yawn, he settled comfortably alongside, and they both fell asleep.

Kabir woke up as he heard loud voices outside the truck. He realised that the truck's engine had been turned off and it was standing still. He nudged Reeya awake, signalling her at the same time to be quiet.

Looking at the time, he figured they were close to their destination. This seemed like an unscheduled stop. From a small fissure in the wall of the truck, he could see red and blue flashing lights. *Police cars!* he thought. *Were the police looking for them, or was this an unrelated incident? Could the mercenaries have tracked them?* Kabir realised he was just being paranoid. Nevertheless, he wanted to be ready and pulled out his service gun.

He was relieved when he heard that the altercation was about over-speeding. The cops were refusing to take a bribe and simply wanted to fine the driver for going over the speed limit.

Once the cops allowed the truck to leave, Kabir breathed easier. After all, he too was party to the smuggling. In fact, he was the contraband being smuggled. He told himself he'd address his conscience later.

"Do we know where we are?" Reeya asked.

"I cannot see much that tells me our location, but based on the time we have been travelling, I'd say we have covered about three-quarters of the way," Kabir guessed.

Reeya could see Kabir off and on in the passing light that filtered through the cracks. He was slouched, seemingly comfortably, against the wall of the old truck. She tried slouching the same way, but found it uncomfortable. The thought of leaning against Kabir made her smile. Kabir noticed the smile and smiled back, unaware that Reeya was growing fond of him too.

"Hey, if you are uncomfortable, feel free to lean on my shoulder. I don't bite," he said. And then hurriedly added, "Unless there is a reason you don't want to."

Reeya smiled, but the last sentence made her pause. She moved in close to Kabir, "Well, yes, there is, but that is for me to figure out. Not much anyone can help me with."

"What reason?" asked Kabir in his direct fashion.

Reeya took a pause as she looked at Kabir. Maybe it was his kind eyes, or just the warmth she felt knowing he was next to her, she decided she could open up more. "Before I came to Nalanda, I had a boyfriend in the UK. Technically, I still do. We never officially broke up. Well, I did, but he still seems to think that I'll eventually go back to him. He continues to send me notes and flowers every so often."

"Why did you break up, if I may ask?" Kabir asked curiously.

Reeya found Kabir's interest in her endearing, and with a nervous little laugh replied, "I'm glad you asked. Talking helps me get clarity. I did not feel I could love him the way he deserves. I tried to explain it to him, but I am not sure he understood." Reeya's voice trailed off as she recalled the difficult conversations.

In a stronger voice, she continued, "I did not see a future with him. I was not enamoured with his traditional thinking, and I don't see monetary success as the only goal. I feel success is perceived differently by different people. I find peace in engaging with our ancient history and success in demystifying it. I felt my calling was here."

"You seem to take a lot of pride in our ancient history," observed Kabir.

Reeya reflected on his comment before replying with a little laugh, "It's interesting that you see it that way. I believe in humility. Pride is so overrated. If anything, we should take pride in what we have personally achieved, not just by association with a culture or organisation that we happen to belong to. I just find inspiration in our history.

"We accomplished a lot back then, and continue to do so today. A pity that most people are unaware of both. If people knew what made us a success as a society, we would be inspired to do so much more." Reeya continued.

"We tend to epitomise the point in history where it peaked before something caused it to decline. We need to better understand the reasons behind the prosperity and the collapse. I feel that we should take our ancient achievements as an inspiration and drive forward. If we would just inculcate the lessons they left behind, we could reach heights which we would have achieved, if we had not been interrupted." Kabir could sense the passion in Reeya's tone.

"Wow! That was deep," was all that Kabir could say as he processed what Reeya had been saying.

"And so, you came here to Nalanda to work with the professor, leaving behind the world you had made for yourself in the UK?" Kabir asked.

"Yeah. It is all behind me, now that I think of it." Reeya said with a distant look. The deep sigh somehow signalled that she was feeling free of the baggage she was carrying.

And with that freedom, she allowed herself to lean against Kabir. The heat and humidity were no match for the sense of security and comfort she felt. Kabir leaned his head back against the truck wall and smiled to himself, enjoying their closeness in silence.

Before long, the truck stopped for fuel and food. Having eaten the packed food, Kabir and Reeya were not hungry. But they needed to stretch their legs.

Kabir decided to call Nair and find out how far the dragnet was spread. He negotiated his way through the cartons and jumped off the truck to a small shop selling refreshments, cigarettes, candies, and such. These shops were common on the highway and near petrol stations.

His training as a covert operative made it easy for him to pickpocket a cell phone from an unsuspecting customer at the shop. The man had just finished talking on his cell phone and, without locking it, had put it in his pocket. As he called Nair, Kabir fully expected the call to be listened to and traced.

"Sir, I just wanted to let you know that we are safe and continuing with our mission." Not wanting to beat around the bush, he used no names or locations as he continued, "I suspect there is a leak."

"Yes, I realise that. This is bigger than I thought, and I'm trying to get to the bottom of it. But for now, you are on your own and one of the most wanted persons in the country," Nair said, confirming that he was aware of the situation. "I'm talking to the chief and getting the record straightened. But you need to stay safe until that is done."

Slipping the cell phone back in the pocket of its rightful owner, Kabir slowly walked back towards the truck. He knew the cell phone location would be traced, and this unsuspecting customer would be questioned somewhere along the highway. But he would not have any answers to provide, and no descriptions to give. Kabir was hoping the whole exercise would take long enough for them to disappear.

Reeya was stretching her hamstring against the back of the truck. "What did you find?" She asked curiously.

"Nothing that we did not already know or suspect. We are the most wanted people in the country right now. Nair is trying to figure out a way. But till that happens, we need to lie low."

"How could this have happened?" Reeya asked incredulously.

It forced Kabir to give it a deeper thought. He knew the chief very well. The chief also knew Kabir, and there was no way the chief would be party to this manhunt.

Who is orchestrating it, and how did this happen without his knowledge? The thought was now beginning to gnaw at Kabir as they both got back into the truck and headed to Udaipur.

12
Udaipur

Day 3 | 0600 hrs

THE TRUCK MADE A SLIGHT DETOUR OFF THE HIGHWAY TO STOP at a nearby petrol pump. The driver got down and knocked on the back of the truck. Kabir and Reeya got off, looking their part as two lovers eloping in their traditional wedding garb.

"This is as far as we can bring you. Now we must drop the shipment, and the boss said he didn't want you anywhere near that," said the driver, wishing them luck as he drove away.

Pointing towards the city, Kabir said, "It's a bit of a walk, but I know a person who can help us there." Reeya nodded and started to walk.

"Kabir, this footwear won't do." She was referring to her slippers and, looking at Kabir, burst out laughing. "And yours won't either. I don't see you being able to walk for long in those shoes." Leather *juttis* were not meant for soft city feet.

"He really dressed you up like a labourer about to get married," Reeya continued laughing as she could now see him in properly. Kabir wanted to point out that she was dressed to match, but seeing how the dress added to her sensuality, he held back and just smiled as they made their way through the slush caused by the monsoon rains.

"We will have to put shopping on our agenda now, won't we?" Kabir continued, holding back his own laughter. "I should take a picture of you to show you how well Yassir has dressed you up—my bride-to-be!

"Shall we make our way to the city now? You also mentioned wanting to meet the dean of Poorvi University?" Kabir asked, more like a statement than a question.

"Yes, it is a premier institute, and the archaeology department is well respected. We may learn something. It is probably nearby as it is located on the outskirts of the city," Reeya said.

Kabir and Reeya made their way towards the city, avoiding the slushy patches on the pavement. Kabir was looking for an appropriate place to ask for directions to Poorvi Vidyapeeth, when Reeya pointed to the large sign on the boundary wall of a campus.

"Poorvi Vidyapeeth?" Reeya read out aloud with an expression of relief in her eyes. It seemed serendipitous that they should happen to reach the one place they could potentially find some answers.

"Dr Narendra Khosla. That's his name. I think we should go meet him. I know they have faculty housing on campus," Reeya recalled her last encounter. Pausing to look at her attire, she added, "But, like this?"

Kabir paused to consider the likely outcomes of meeting Dr Khosla. But he realised they had no answers and a lot of questions, including what it was that someone wanted badly enough to commit murder for. Dr Khosla seemed to be the only likely source they had at this point.

Kabir and Reeya walked up to the entrance of the university, where they spotted a watchman standing guard. "If we go through the gate, he will ask us for identification. Let's go from the back entry. It is closer to the faculty housing."

It took them some time to circle around the large campus to reach the back gate. It looked like a service entrance and was unmanned at this early hour. The two were easily able to walk to the cluster of buildings that looked like the faculty housing.

"Who are you looking for?" a watchman heading to the back gate on an antique-looking bicycle enquired.

"Khosla *ji* needed some work done and had called for some labour," Reeya replied, assuming a rustic accent.

"Yes, the plumbing system has been acting up in that building," the watchman said, pointing to the last building. "Go to the second floor. His door is the one in blue," The guard instructed, assuming they wouldn't be able to read numbers. With a colloquial word of thanks, Reeya gestured to Kabir to follow her.

Dr Khosla, seemingly not yet fully awake, walked up to the front door as he rubbed his greying beard. He was not expecting two labourers dressed up as a bride and groom to show up so early in the morning. He was even more surprised when Reeya reminded him of their meeting in Rajgir with Professor Ghosh.

"Yes, I remember. The professor spoke so highly of you. Come in, come in." He stepped aside to let them in. "What are you doing here, and why on earth are you dressed like this?"

He gestured to a couple of chairs and suggested they first have some tea and freshen up. He then turned to his helper, who stood in the adjoining kitchen doorway. "Make *chai* for them. And some breakfast. And then pack my lunch."

It looked like a well-kept, cosy two-bedroom apartment. They were both glad for the air conditioning that finally gave them a break from the humid weather outside. Kabir and Reeya sat adjacent to each other at the small dining table, with Dr Khosla across from them.

Kabir noticed a retort, like the one in Reeya's bag, sitting under a spotlight in the corner of the living room. It was tastefully displayed with other artefacts. The house was quite modern, unlike the archaic house of Professor Ghosh that Kabir had visited the day before.

Dr Khosla heard their story with interest as they finished their *chai*. Reeya took the retort out and placed it gently on the table. Dr Khosla examined it gingerly.

"So, the professor managed to get himself into trouble after all," Dr Khosla said to no one in particular. "We had talked about it, and I did warn him not to mess with the legend. Yes, there is a legend. But it is only that. A legend." He was looking at the etched binary numbers on the retort.

"What legend?" Kabir asked curiously, while Reeya just waited patiently.

Laughing, Dr Khosla tried to downplay what he had just said. "Well, there are many. It would be hard to figure out which one of them the professor was following. But I will tell you what I know."

He paused and then continued. "Obviously, the professor getting killed means there was more to it. Which is worrisome. But it does not necessarily mean that the legend is true. Maybe parts of it are, or maybe someone believes it is true."

Kabir was on the edge of his seat. He really wanted to learn more. *What else did the professor know that he hadn't even hinted about?* They seemed to be accumulating clues with every passing hour.

"To begin with, there's a lot more to our history than you would have learnt in school," Dr Khosla settled back into his chair. "If a common man is asked to pick examples of our historical monuments, it is quite likely that they would pick the Taj Mahal or the Red Fort. But both those monuments were constructed in the relatively recent past, within the last 500 years or so.

"These were made just before our GDP started to decline—from about 25 per cent of the world's GDP for thousands of years, to a mere 4 per cent and declining when we became a free nation again[108]. What is interesting, and is not widely known, is what economic and commercial activities caused and sustained the GDP at such high levels for thousands of years before the sudden decline in the 1700s. How was the society so productive?"

It wasn't the first time Kabir had heard about the pre-colonial prosperity and the rapid decline of the Indian economy as a colonised nation. "So, what exactly did we do for our GDP to be the largest in the world?" Kabir was curious.

"I don't recall learning about anything other than spices and textiles. But I feel there was a lot more that contributed to the prosperity of ancient India. I have heard of references to untold riches in our scriptures like Ramayana and such, but there is no mention of the activities that brought about such prosperity."

With a satisfied grunt, Dr Khosla continued, "Yes, we have been taught to memorise history but not to investigate the facts. Though I see a change in the current generation. We are starting to question again and moving towards a more scientific approach, not very different from ancient times. I believe it was this very approach to question and understand, and improve that drove our industrial output. Be it mining, metallurgy, cotton textiles or even knowledge and ideas. All this and more brought in the wealth that India became famous for.

"The number system was likely invented out of need because of this sprawling trade with other contemporary civilisations, starting with the Mesopotamian and the Egyptian, followed by the Greek, the Chinese, the Roman and the others that came later. Unfortunately, despite the ancient Indian civilisation being one of the larger and more complex ones, it occupies little space in textbooks or famous museums compared to its contemporaries," lamented Dr Khosla.

"The Indian civilisation is also celebrated for its philosophical efflorescence. There were several high philosophical traditions within both Hinduism and Buddhism. However, there was also an esoteric yogic tradition that developed in both religions, privileging secretive occultist practices. Dr Ghosh was researching the existence of three such occultist sects that span several centuries. There are no written records to corroborate their existence, and many consider that they were simply figments of the imagination of later writers."

"There were probably many such secret societies we'll never really know about. Some were home-grown, and some even had connections to neighbouring cultures. If we assume that the Heliodorus pillar was important to them, the Cult of Serapis or the deadlier Companion Cavalry come to mind. Let me emphasise that we cannot be certain that they even existed, let alone attribute anything to them."

"But we can make some hypotheses," Dr Khosla seemed to be enjoying deviating from his regular history lectures. "Both of these were rumoured to have had a hand in Alexander's death. Whether they were protecting him or conspiring against him is uncertain."

"It sounds interesting. Wasn't Alexander in India around 327-326 BCE?" Kabir had obviously been paying attention, and seeing him get better with the timelines made Reeya smile.

"A fragment or more of either, or both of these societies, may well be active today and could be behind the death of the professor," Dr Khosla announced ominously.

Kabir reflected on the resources of the mercenaries he was up against and asked the question, the answer to which had proved most elusive, "But what are they after?"

"It is hard to tell. Several treasures or coveted objects come to mind," Dr Khosla said pensively and continued to elaborate. "You know, not too long ago, they found hidden gold and precious metals worth billions, if not trillions of US Dollars, in Padmanabhaswamy temple in Kerala[109]. So, if they are after simple cash-hoards, several sites still remain undiscovered. Son Bhandar Caves—Bimbisara's treasury—are empty today, but were rumoured to have been overflowing with gold and silver. It can be found if you can decipher the script in the caves.

"Another one is King Kothi—the palace of the Nizam of Hyderabad, who was one of the wealthiest individuals of all time. The Nizam was so wealthy that he was portrayed on the cover of *Time* magazine in 1937, being described as the world's richest man at the time. At its peak, his fortune was estimated to be $2 billion, equivalent to about $236 billion today after adjusting it for inflation based on keeping the same proportion of US GDP.[110] It is rumoured that a large piece of it is still missing.

"But these are just treasures of large monetary value," Dr Khosla shuffled in his chair, turning his attention to other items the mercenaries could be after. "My hunch is that they're after something even bigger. Since the mercenaries are foreigners, what if the hunt is not for anything of Indian origin? Hear me out. It is rumoured that the Ark of the Covenant was smuggled into India and has been kept here safely since. It contains the original tablets engraved with the Ten Commandments. And while history tells us otherwise, there are also unsubstantiated rumours that Alexander's body was cremated in India and the remains were buried with his sword and the chalice of immortality, which he wisely chose not to drink from.

"My best guess, and bear in mind that it is only a guess, is..." continued Dr Khosla with a level of finality. "They are looking for the Tomb of Alexander to find the chalice. Mind you, the story about Alexander's remains being buried in India could well be a myth."

"But we know where he is buried, and it is not in India. And why now?" Reeya burst out in protest, finding Dr Khosla's arguments devoid of substance.

"Slow down. Let's take your questions one at a time," Dr Khosla said calmly. "Let's take the sequence of the clues you have followed so far. Starting from Nalanda, you were led to a Jain cave. Which led you to a Greek pillar and in turn brought you to Zawar."

Dr Khosla seemed to be stitching together something that Kabir and Reeya hoped would make some sense to them. "Alexander spent eighteen to nineteen months in India. This includes crossing the Hindukush, his stay in Taxila, the battle of Jhelum, and his retirement from the area after his battle-weary army revolted[111]. It is said that his elite unit of handpicked soldiers, known as the Companion Cavalry, tried to assassinate him as he turned back towards Greece. But he didn't turn back immediately, and no one really knows what he was doing here in the interim.

"In fact, it was female spies and warriors who kept him safe as he searched for the chalice of immortality. We don't know if he ever discovered what he set out to find, but we do know he had accumulated clues for it," Dr Khosla said, wrapping up his theory.

His theory seemed quite far-fetched to Reeya and Kabir, but then, there was a well-trained band of mercenaries looking for something and given how little they knew, no theories could be discounted. Maybe it was the tomb, or maybe it wasn't. For now, they were as much in the dark as when they had entered Dr Khosla's apartment.

Dr Khosla reached for the retort that Reeya had placed on the table with an inquiring look towards Reeya and Kabir. "May I?" Kabir and Reeya nodded in unison, eager to learn more about it.

Dr Khosla took the retort to the kitchen sink and proceeded to wash away any dirt still clinging to it under the cold water faucet. He then dried it with a kitchen towel, dabbing the mouth carefully. Wrapping the towel around his finger, he proceeded to clean the inside of the neck, as far as he could reach. He rotated it till the light fell straight into the neck and he could see inside.

"The neck is sealed," concluded Dr Khosla. "It is never sealed, as in the normal process, the zinc needs to pour out of the neck. This retort has been modified to conceal something inside. I'm sorry, but we will need to break it open."

Reeya was on the verge of protesting, but held back as she realised there was no other way of knowing what was inside. Dr Khosla went to a nearby drawer and took out a triangular file. He proceeded to neatly etch a straight line around the neck and then made the groove deeper by going over it again. Holding the neck in one hand and the body in the other, he gently applied pressure as the retort split into two along the groove. Dr Khosla put his fingers in and pulled out a neatly stitched crimson cloth.

"The root of *Majeeth*, or the red dye. It is made from the root of *Rubia cordifolia*, or *Majeeth*. The ancients used it to dye cloth. It contains purpurin,"[112] Dr Khosla identified. "These days, they are trying to use purpurin in lithium-ion batteries. But its earliest known use dates back to the first millennium BCE as a cotton dye[113]. It is believed to have antimicrobial properties[114] and was thought to prevent documents wrapped in it from deteriorating," Dr Khosla explained.

From the cloth, he extracted a bundle of palm leaves neatly strung together with thread. Reeya and Kabir found themselves marvelling at what seemed to be an ancient handwritten manuscript.

Reeya reached out with both hands, instinctively wanting to hold it. Ever so delicately, she began perusing the pages. In a reverent whisper, she said, "This is Sanskrit written in an ancient script, likely Nagari.[115]"

"It gives us a timeline, as we know it was developed around the seventh century CE. It is thought to be a precursor to the Devanagari script. [116] We don't see much of it after the 11th century CE," Dr Khosla said, pulling a hardbound book from his bookshelf and turning the pages. "Here, even though the alphabets are similar to today's Devanagari script, this table may be useful for you to read the script."

After careful examination and with the help of the translation table provided by Khosla, she explained, "The initial part invokes various gods and offers prayers to those writing and reading these pages." Reeya pushed ahead, gingerly turning the palm leaves. She had expected them to be very brittle with age, but surprisingly, they were still intact.

"*The invaders are seeking and destroying much of the secrets and knowledge gained over time. We, the* vishkanyas, *have guarded this secret for centuries. The cauldron must be first understood before it can be brought to the world—it must be kept safe but not uncovered until humanity is ready for it.*"

"*Vishkanya*?" Reeya read out in amazement. "Were they real?" Reeya had always wanted to put a name to the female warriors she had seen on the Sanchi Stupa. Despite her historian-self telling her otherwise, she was making a connection between the stone carvings and the characters of the manuscript.

"So the rumour that Alexander was kept alive by female spies and warriors may be true after all!" mused Dr Khosla.

"There is nothing here that says anything about Alexander, and it does not say what these women did," Reeya pointed out to Dr Khosla, drawing a clear line between what the ancient manuscript said and wishful thinking.

The three continued trying to read and decipher, but nothing else stood out as useful to them. Kabir and Reeya still did not know why a cauldron would be such a big secret, or why a group calling itself *vishkanyas* was trying to protect it. They could only hope that this information was going to be more useful than the musings of Dr Khosla, which Reeya had mostly dismissed as myths at best.

"And we still don't know the hiding place of the cauldron, or why a team of mercenaries is killing people to get to it," Kabir observed as he realised that they did not seem any closer to knowing what they were looking for or how to get to it.

All three paused at the sound of the loud thunder. They were so absorbed in the manuscript that none of them had noticed when it started pouring heavily outside. The torrential onslaught and dark skies evoked a familiar feeling of dread and nostalgia.

"Why don't you go freshen up. Hopefully, by that time, it would have stopped raining," suggested Dr Khosla.

"These are my daughter's. I think they will fit you," he told Reeya, handing her some clothes. And then, turning to Kabir, "See if you can use some of my clothes for now."

After they had changed, Dr Khosla offered, "I can drop you off at the city. But be careful to go only to the small shops, as all the large malls have CCTV cameras everywhere that are well monitored."

Day 3 | 1100 hrs

Reeya was carrying her backpack, replenished with food and napkins, and both pieces of the neatly cut retort. The palm-leaf manuscript, wrapped in its red cloth covering, was back in the larger half of the earthen retort, alongside the mystical wootz fragment.

Dr Khosla drove the small car through the narrow streets. "I'll drop you off near the shopping street," Dr Khosla said as the torrential downpour continued. "You should meet the interim lead historian at Zawar. He can tell you more about the history of the mines and guide you to what you are looking for.

"He usually makes a trip to the site the day before and goes to his office at 5 pm, at the end of his day. He is there for an hour before he heads home," Dr Khosla said, speaking loudly to be heard over the din made by the downpour.

The drumming of the rain subsided as they pulled under a makeshift canopy installed for the convenience of the shoppers being dropped off. Speaking softly, he said, "Best of luck to both of you. I hope I get to see you again. Feel free to reach out as and when you need to."

Kabir and Reeya waved at Dr Khosla as he pulled away. While they were thankful for the clothes provided by him, they headed to the nearest shop to get something more comfortable. Kabir was glad to get back into comfortable shoes and jeans. And Reeya picked up a dark-blue *kurta*, thinking it would be better suited to hiding in the shadows if necessary.

"Now to meet Raghvendra. Well, Kunwar Raghvendra," said Kabir in a low voice. He pointed to the next sheltered spot, and they dashed to it while the rain was light. They kept moving from shelter to shelter through the narrow street to avoid the drizzle.

"We should have picked up a couple of umbrellas, too," Reeya said as she realised the obvious missed opportunity.

"We are almost there," Kabir reassured her as they made yet another short dash to the canopy of a fruit vendor.

The rain had stopped, and they found themselves walking along the banks of Lake Pichola. Kabir stopped to take in the view of the distant hills with the shimmering water and a magnificent floating palace in the foreground. Even though the local *Ahar-Banas* Culture dates back to 3000 BCE or earlier[117], the rulers of Mewar that came later had done a splendid job of using the natural beauty of the area to their best advantage in building their palaces and monuments. They continued their walk on the curved pathway and approached a palatial residence overlooking the lake. It looked regal with its turrets, arched gates, and symmetrical front gardens.

"Let's go through the back," suggested Kabir. Reeya nodded and felt like she knew the drill by now. Going in through the service entrance and walking through the kitchen, Kabir and Reeya reached the formal living area.

An opulent 20-feet-tall chandelier hanging off the high domed ceiling gave the room a majestic feel. The carefully selected artefacts and paintings of men in regal attire added to the richness of the space. Walking past a large ceramic sculpture that a world-class artist seemed to have been commissioned to make, they reached the rich teak wooden doors of the study.

Kunwar, as the title implied, was the prince of the estate, and his personality reflected it well. Young at heart, Kunwar Raghvendra obviously still enjoyed a fast-paced video game on the large-screen console. Reeya and Kabir couldn't understand the game, but could see his deep involvement by the aggressive manoeuvring of the controls.

"Hello Raghvendra!" Judging from the familiarity in Kabir's tone, Reeya realised Kabir obviously knew the prince and knew him well.

"Kabir! My friend! What brings you here?" Raghvendra seemed pleasantly surprised as he fidgeted with the console to pause the game.

"By the way, when I said my house is your house, I did mean it, but not that you can just walk in without ringing the doorbell," he said with a smile that had a tinge of displeasure.

"And who do we have here? Are you escorting her to the Miss Universe pageant?" Raghvendra asked, turning his attention to Reeya, theatrically bowing over her hand and kissing it. "You do know that I am organising the pageant this year, right? And it's going to redefine opulence. And not just in this part of the world." Obviously, Raghvendra didn't feel much need for modesty.

"Good to see you too, Raghvendra. Looks like you are doing well and may not need to be rescued again," an allusion to a history between them that instantly turned Raghvendra from an over-the-top royal to a grateful and warm friend.

"What do you need, Kabir? You know it is all at your disposal," Kunwar Raghvendra said, magnanimously offering his help.

"For now, just a car. I may need more help soon. Have you heard?" Kabir did not need to finish the sentence as he saw Raghvendra nodding vigorously.

"Yes, and I don't know what is going on, but if you tell me, I may be able to help you with more than just a car. You can trust me now," Raghvendra said with a smile, returning to his jovial self. "I have not done anything that I have hidden from you, at least not since you saved my skin four years ago. Pinky promise." Kabir had kept tabs on Raghvendra and knew that he was telling the truth.

Kabir decided to give Raghvendra a summarised version of events, focusing on the murder of the professor. He also mentioned being chased by a gang of mercenaries led by Myra.

"Hmmm… Myra," Raghvendra paused as he wanted to see the look on Kabir's face. "A car is the least of your problems, my friend. As I had promised, I don't support any criminal activity on Indian soil. That was our deal, and I have honoured it." He wanted to make sure he clarified that before Kabir jumped to any conclusions about Raghvendra's involvement.

"She did approach me with her shopping list. But I politely declined," Raghvendra said with a poker face.

"Of course, you declined. But I am sure you recommended one of your associates." Kabir knew Raghvendra very well, so he prodded him along. "Which one? And I need to know the details."

"Kabir *ji*," Raghvendra was back to his theatrics. "It was I who asked you if I could help you. And I even informed you about Myra and her shopping list. Even if you don't believe me, I am fully willing to help you get all the details." Raghvendra's theatrics were quite convincing.

"I'm listening," Kabir played along.

"Myra had a very sophisticated shopping list—advanced communication devices, signal jammers, the usual high-end guns and pre-calibrated sniper rifles. She also wanted explosives and a Geiger counter." Raghvendra had his eyes fixed on Kabir as he continued, "The word is she is Ezio's top henchman, or henchperson. I suppose we must be gender-neutral these days."

Kabir had crossed paths with Ezio before. Looking towards Reeya, he realised she was at sea and he needed to share his information with her.

"I know Ezio. He is a ruthless criminal and the mastermind of many heinous crimes. He started out with smuggling antiques, graduating to drugs and human trafficking. Now is an arms dealer that can easily equip a small nation."

"Under the guise of a respectable businessman who plays by the rules, he controls several oil and gas pipelines and shipping routes." His distaste for Ezio could be clearly heard in Kabir's tone as he continued. "If Ezio is involved, it is not good news. As he is usually after something big."

Reeya was wondering what could be so big to warrant Ezio's interest? She was convinced that Dr. Khosla's theory did not make much sense, but mention of a cauldron was gnawing at her.

"We will figure it out," Kabir said, guessing what Reeya was thinking. She turned away, smiling at how in sync they were.

Kabir turned to Raghvendra and muttered a *thanks*, though not a very genuine one.

"You are welcome, Kabir *ji*," Raghvendra said, enjoying having the upper hand on Kabir for once in all their interactions.

He paused and continued in a softer, more sincere tone, "Kabir, I'm very sorry about Vani." It seemed there was more Raghvendra wanted to say on this topic, but he held himself back. Hearing Vani's name, he felt that all too familiar sinking feeling. The sincere condolence mellowed Kabir, who just nodded to thank Raghvendra for the sentiment.

Reeya noticed the sudden change in dynamics but reined in her curiosity for later when she was alone with Kabir. "And the car?"

"Yes, of course. I suggest you take the small SUV. It will be handy with the rain and slush. It is clean—that is, minus a GPS. So it will not be trackable by me or anyone else. Do please return it in good shape," Raghvendra said pleadingly, obviously recalling some more of his shared history with Kabir.

"And as a gesture of goodwill, I'll add a small picnic bag of goodies you may need," Raghvendra said magnanimously.

Kabir knew the goodies were things that would keep them alive in case of trouble—a handgun, and probably a few burner phones. He nodded his appreciation as they walked towards the SUV.

Kabir took a camera phone out of the neatly packed case and handed it to Reeya to replace the phone he had tossed when being chased by Myra.

13

Zawar

Day 3 | 1500 hrs

KABIR LIKED THE FEEL OF THE RELATIVELY SMALL BUT POWERFUL SUV as he navigated around water puddles through the side streets. They were southbound on the smooth highway to Zawar.

"What happened between you and Raghvendra? I could sense some old animosity," Reeya asked curiously.

"I did wreck a car of his once, if that is what you are asking. But I guess you want to know the story leading up to it," he smiled, giving her a quick glance.

"In all fairness, he was dealt a lousy set of cards. He inherited a debt-laden estate when his parents died a few years back. Raghvendra tried to rescue the estate by gunrunning across some international borders. He managed a couple of runs, but then one of his suppliers double-crossed him. Raghvendra could have died in that operation." Kabir was giving Reeya the broad outlines without going into the details.

"Let's just say, it was lucky for him that I was there to take down the other party. Raghvendra escaped, but on being apprehended, swore that he had never done anything illegal on Indian soil, so he could not be arrested in India." Kabir paused and smiled. "He also claimed I could not arrest him on foreign soil as it was outside my jurisdiction.

"He may or may not have been right, but he did help me get one of my injured teammates to the hospital. Raghvendra saved his life, but in the process, his car got wrecked." Kabir thought for a moment and continued. "I let him go as he was not my target, but I know he managed to keep a small fortune in the process.

"I think I always knew he had connections and that they would be useful someday. And he has been providing us with good intel, off and on. I'd call him an informant and leave it at that," Kabir concluded.

Reeya's gaze softened, and she leaned in with a mildly appreciative smile as she listened with interest. But it didn't answer one question, a very important one, given what was developing between Kabir and her. "Who is Vani? Raghvendra mentioned her back there. What happened to her?"

She saw Kabir wince as he drifted back to the past. "It's been a while," he started, trying to make the moment more comfortable. Then, in a rush, "She was everything to me. I met her when she was still finishing her studies." Reeya sensed the pauses were corresponding to incidents he was recalling.

"We hit it off very well, and I'm not sure when it happened, but we fell deeply in love. It changed my life. She became my inspiration." With a change of tone, he suddenly burst out, "Well, till I found out that her dad was my boss!" He laughed at the memory.

"She could handle any situation with calmness and grace, and helped me negotiate the tumultuous feelings I was going through," Kabir said and then paused as the painful memory replayed in his mind.

"She died in an explosion that was meant to kill me," Kabir said, his resolute expression clearly indicating that he would eventually find those responsible.

Reeya could feel his sadness as he spoke of Vani. Her hand instinctively reached out to cover his on the gear shift. Kabir felt the touch, and the smile returned to his face, the vengeful expression fading. He turned his hand so he could take hold of hers.

"How has Rajgir been for you?"

"It was difficult initially, and I missed Arjun. But then, I got engrossed in work and found it very satisfying. With time, my passion for the work took over. In India, we mix myth and folklore with history, and just separating them and finding evidence to back everything has been an incredible experience. I like my new independent lifestyle and my ability to contribute to our understanding of our own history," Reeya said contentedly.

Kabir could relate to what Reeya was saying as he, too, had found passion in his work. Success, as perceived by society, was not his driving force.

Drawing parallels in his mind, he tried to stitch it all up in a sentence: "I find my meaning in protecting what you so passionately discover." Reeya found it oddly relatable and giggled at the thought.

"Yes, you can say that, I suppose." She suddenly became aware that they had been holding hands all this while and was overcome by a feeling of self-consciousness.

Kabir sensed her awkwardness and let go of her hand as he changed gears. He made a left turn onto a narrow road, lined with green shrubs and trees, that would take them towards Zawar. As they drove, they could see some ancient temple ruins along the way.

"Most of these are ancient temples frequented by the locals. Once upon a time, this area was a bustling centre of activity and commerce. I had originally wanted to do my thesis in this general location as it could possibly have been impacted by the changing course of the now vanished Sarswati river[118]," Reeya said, explaining her familiarity with the region.

She pointed to a cluster of green hills that seemed to be cut on one side. "See those hills? They are the ones I told you about, created by the spent ore and broken retorts piled up over thousands of years. You can see the astounding number of retorts from the area that is exposed in the cut. Can you imagine how much zinc would have been distilled here?"

"Wow! What did they do with all that zinc? There must have been tons of it!" Kabir was trying to imagine the scale of industrialisation that must have existed around these man-made hills.

"Can we stop there? Near the hill. I'll show you what the remains look like," suggested Reeya.

Kabir was also curious and found a convenient place to park off the highway. Reeya went towards a small hill that had a section broken off. It was a rather steep climb, but Reeya went up with ease and kneeled over to pick up some debris.

"See this?" Reeya showed Kabir what seemed like an earthen baked container. "It is a piece of one of the millions of retorts that were used here to distil zinc. It still contains the spent ore." Reeya was pointing to the dirt inside, at the bottom of the earthen pot.

"Wow!" Kabir was at a loss for words. "I can imagine a village with several families. Some members shaped the soil into a container, while others baked it. Maybe they got the kids to fill it up with ore, and then the older people attached the funnel at the top of the retort with clay and baked it again."

Kabir was imagining the assembly line made up of friends and families, living in harmony. They spent their day working and likely considered it their *dharma*. He visualised an open-minded culture that encouraged innovation and put in sincere efforts. He wondered if the *Bhagavad Gita's* core teaching of *Karmanyevadhikaraste*—put in your sincere efforts—was simply a sum of the essence of the culture in what we now call as golden years of the Indian civilisation.

A deviation from this simple tenet is held by some to be a root cause of the decline of the civilisation. Eventually, it led to the colonisation of a people who had led what could be termed the original industrial revolution. "Do we know how old this is?" Kabir asked Reeya.

"We have conjectures." Reeya tilted her head as she fumbled for an answer. "They probably started mining zinc here as early as 500 BCE, using open mines[119]. It was mixed with copper to make brass. Initially, they were mixing the ore, but a few hundred years later, they were, most likely, using the zinc distilled from the ore, which allowed for a much higher quality brass. We would need to dig to the bottom of these hills to carbon-date the older artefacts. Living here in 3000 BCE, you would have been a part of the *Ahar-Banas* rural culture before they started mining.

"And what you are holding in your hand could be about 2000 years old," Reeya said, pointing to the somewhat intact retort that Kabir was examining.

Their gaze met momentarily as they both looked up from the retort and at each other. The attraction between them was evident, but both pretended to be unaware of it. And yet, they were thankful to be together.

"Let's go and meet the interim-in-charge, Dr Khosla mentioned. It is almost five and he'll reach his office soon," Kabir said, the broken retorts reminding him of why they were there in the first place.

"Yes. Let's go," Reeya said, lowering her gaze and adding with some humour, "We have a murder to solve and a world to save."

"Captain Kabir and the intrepid historian Reeya to the rescue!" Kabir declared playing along as they got into the car and resumed their drive to the Zawar mines.

~

He found parking near the office building of the interim-in-charge of archaeological operations. Walking up the steps of the porch, Kabir saw some exhibits and the write-ups alongside. He realised that while the mines are now leased to a private company, they were indeed the longest-running mines in history. He noticed a replica of the ancient furnace used for smelting. Seeing it gave him a better sense of what it must have taken for this to be done on an industrial scale. He excitedly pointed it out to Reeya. While several pictures and replicas were placed at the entrance, He felt it was a meagre homage to an astounding achievement of mankind, but a homage, nevertheless.

The guard at the gate asked them for identification to write their names in the entry register. It was a common practice in most large establishments to ensure transparency of visitors to the officers.

More vestigial practices that we need to address at some point in time, thought Kabir, questioning, as many did in the younger generation, archaic practices that have been allowed to continue without asking *why*.

Kabir wrote down fictitious names and simply 'meeting' as the reason under 'purpose of visit'. The guard who was perhaps at the end of his shift or perhaps, knowing the futility of the practice, didn't give it a second glance. He dutifully pointed out the room of the interim-in-charge for Kabir and Reeya to head to.

The name plate mounted on the door just said 'Interim-in-Charge of Archaeological section'. "Doesn't he have a name?" Reeya said to Kabir's amusement, "Or does his wife also call him 'interim-in-charge' when he gets home?"

"Hello. You must be the superintendent of police, and you, the historian that Dr Khosla rang about." An athletic man, barely in his 30s, but balding, walked towards the two. The interim-in-charge also seemed to know them by their titles.

"Hello. Yes, I'm Ajit and this is Sunita," Kabir said, giving the fictitious names he had filled in the register.

Reeya looked at him, incredulously mouthing the word, *Sunita? Seriously? You couldn't think of anything better? Sunita?*

"Why does your nameplate say interim?" Reeya asked, suppressing a smile. "Will it eventually change to permanent?"

"My name is Eegaiarasu Chiranjeev Gunasekaran. Please call me ECG for short," said the interim-in-charge with a smile. "And not likely, to answer your question. I am on loan from the archaeology department. When they hire someone for this position, they will change the nameplate. But they are not in a rush to hire anyone, so I think I'll retire as the interim-in-charge," ECG said with a comical expression.

Kabir could see Reeya stifling a laugh and signalled to her with a slight shake of the head to control the urge.

"ECG *ji*", Kabir said in a serious tone, but realising it sounded ridiculous, made another attempt, "Gunasekaran *ji*, did Dr Khosla tell you what we are looking for?"

"Yes, he did," ECG, thankfully oblivious to Reeya's reaction to his name, answered politely.

"So, what did he tell you?" Kabir asked, realising after a long pause that ECG needed to be prodded to elicit a complete answer.

"He said that I should guide you to the old section of the mine. Keep in mind that they are dangerous and closed to the public. He also mentioned that this was being done in the national interest and I should assist as best as I can." ECG replied. Then added in a helpful tone, "Even so, I would not advise you to enter the mines. But, since I don't think you will take my advice, I do have some torches for you to take along."

Reeya was listening with a big grin on her face as she found the interaction rather comical.

"And what may we find there?" Kabir continued his inquiry, ignoring her ill-timed mirth.

"Most of the things we find during an excavation, we send to the museum. The mines are several levels deep, but do not contain any artefacts. Other than some inscriptions in Brahmi, there is little of value in there."

Gesturing with his arms, ECG pointed straight ahead. "It's about one kilometre from here. We can just walk there if it is not raining."

The rain had stopped, and even though it was humid, it was cool enough to walk. The three stepped out and walked eastwards. The small bridge across a seasonal stream was under repair. The monsoon rains had caused the stream to swell, and it would have been quite unsafe to try crossing it on foot. They decided to take the service bridge a little further north.

There is still enough daylight left for us to go in and come back. Hopefully, it won't take us that long in the mines, Kabir thought to himself.

Even though the working mines with the little villages didn't make for a great view to their right, they had a beautiful green hill to their left. It took a little over ten minutes for them to reach a rock garden.

"It's just a little ahead from here," was ECG's reading as they walked, treading carefully.

"As you may know, the Zawar mines were the first to produce zinc[120], which made it possible for the world to make brass. Interestingly, as they learned to distil it, they were initially producing medicinal zinc powder for healing various ailments.[121]" ECG informed the two as they walked.

Soon, they approached a clump of trees with a narrow path leading through them. A small sign, prohibiting entry and warning of potential danger, was barely readable through peeling paint and rusted metal.

They continued on the well-trodden path that was surprisingly not very muddy despite the rain. A small shack stood at the end of the path with a guard posted outside. A metal grill gate lay closed to prevent anyone from entering uninvited.

"You see the fields around the structure? These were the original mines. They are what we call open mines, with the ore easily accessible near the surface." ECG stood with his hands on his hips, surveying the land. Kabir was glad that Reeya had already given him some basic information about the history of the mines.

"As they depleted the open mines, they had to dig deeper to start mining. You will see many spots that have been dug vertically along the veins of the rocks to extract the richest portions.[122]" ECG continued, "They also found precious stones and other metals as they dug, possibly some gold and silver. Though not in large quantities, as far as we can tell." He was doing a good job of giving Reeya and Kabir the pulse of the land in ancient times.

Approaching the metal grill, ECG spoke to the guard, explaining the need to enter the mines.

The metal grill was unlocked, and the guard pulled it aside to let them enter. Kabir wondered why they didn't just lock the gates instead of stationing a guard. *Generating employment, I guess.* He entered the structure behind Reeya, realising that she liked taking the lead at historical sites.

"Watch out for the bats!" Kabir joked with Reeya, who turned back to smile at him.

ECG followed, turning on the lights to illuminate the floor. Going further in, he switched on some more lights that lit up the staircase and the floors below. A large ceiling light illuminated the mining shaft. Standing at the top, Kabir could see the stairs narrowing as they went down.

Reeya and Kabir took a moment to admire the sophistication of the ancient mines.

"The wooden support structure you see was added during a later phase. It enabled the miners to go deep into a shaft to mine for the ore used in smelting. It is quite amazing that the wood has survived all this time. We carbon dated it to the 1st Century CE,[123]" said ECG, glad to be sharing his knowledge.

"How deep does this go?" Kabir enquired. He could see the floor at the bottom at about a three or four-floor height, but he wanted to know if there was another shaft that went deeper.

"That is about as deep as it goes, I'd say fifty feet. They also mined sideways at each level," ECG replied, pointing to the dark open spaces behind the doorways that were formed by wooden or stone columns. Kabir could appreciate the scale of the enterprise and the innovative technology that had allowed access to the minerals.

Reeya was the first to descend into the shaft. The air was much more humid there than outside. The musty smell inside indicated that the area had been lying closed, without circulation, for a long time.

Close behind, Kabir was admiring the columns that were holding up the mines. "It's ingenious the way they have spaced out the stone and wooden columns. It sure has stood the test of time. That's more than I can say for some of our newer structures."

Soon they were at the bottom of the shaft. The air seemed heavier, but it was now cooler. Though beads of sweat were now appearing on their foreheads, as the humidity was high.

"This is just as bad as getting drenched in the rain," Reeya said exasperatedly, feeling her soaked *kurta* clinging uncomfortably to her body.

The light had been enough to allow them to see their way into the shaft, but she couldn't see too far ahead now. Turning on her torch, she asked, "Which way from here?"

ECG turned on his torch too, and pointing deeper into the cave, said, "This way. There is a section there that has been preserved. It has a wall covered with writing and sketches that you can take a look at."

The ground was hard, and despite seepage from various parts of the cave, it was not muddy. Reeya attributed the rammed earth under her feet to years of foot traffic from the ancient miners.

"Was there any mechanised process for hoisting the ore out of the shaft?" she asked ECG.

"Hard to say for sure, as any ropes that would have been used in the process would not have lasted all this time. We did find wooden remains to suggest that there was a pulley system to pull up the ore. Of course, it would have involved human or animal effort, but again, without evidence, it can only be considered conjecture at best," ECG answered.

Reeya, by now, was leading the group. She spotted a small opening towards the far end of one of the chambers. Bending down to peer in, she realised she was looking into a narrow, dark tunnel that she couldn't see very far into.

She couldn't see where it led, and its narrowness and depth were making her anxious. She was not claustrophobic, but a tunnel from a chamber more than a millennium old and at least four floors under the surface didn't inspire confidence.

Kabir offered to go in first, but Reeya was not about to let her anxiety get the better of her. Before Kabir could finish his sentence, she was crawling in on all fours. Luckily, it was not a long tunnel, and she reached the other end and called out to them. Kabir followed, and ECG, feeling brave, also decided to venture where he had never been before.

The three stood up and admired the chamber. "A place of worship, perhaps," Reeya said, and her voice echoed softly. They could see an altar at the end of the magnificent chamber, with a path made of uncut stones, leading up to it. On both sides of the path were channels, perhaps for water to flow.

"Do you think this chamber could be booby-trapped, just like in the movies?" ECG tried cracking a joke.

"Those who built it must have frequented it and may even have had some ritualistic ceremony here," Reeya said, pointing to small, raised islets in the channel that had perhaps served as stands for lighting lamps.

The walls were intricately carved with a design that had been much in vogue 2000 years ago. Reeya was quite familiar with it. There was also writing in a script that Kabir was beginning to recognise. He had seen it in Sanchi and on the Heliodorus pillar.

"Brahmi script," he declared proudly, hoping his guess was correct.

Reeya was amused and teased him with a laugh, "Catching up on high school history, finally? Yes, it is Brahmi script."

"But what does it say? No one was taught to read it in high school, you know," Kabir retorted.

"Seems like hymns, from what I can tell. They are not specific to a god but a prayer to nature for continued bounty," Reeya said, trailing off absently as she peered at the alphabet, hoping to find the next clue in them.

The word '*ukku*' caught her attention. Moving closer, she dusted the surface with her hands to make sure and confirmed softly under her breath, "*Ukku.*"

"What does that mean?" Kabir asked impatiently, waiting for Reeya to enlighten him.

Reeya was still trying to read the writing on the wall. As far as Kabir could tell, the words in Brahmi were accompanied by a sketch of an urn, or maybe a cauldron.

Making sure that she had read it accurately, she turned to Kabir to explain. "*Ukku* is an ancient south-Indian word for steel.[124] The same wootz that we found earlier." Reeya thought of the fragment she was still carrying in her bag. "How *ukku* became wootz is a story for another time, but it is a known transformation of the word."

She pulled out the small piece of wootz she had found in the furnace at Nalanda and kept it on her palm. "This fragment seems to be a part of that cauldron," Reeya said, trying to confirm her observation. "But is it the same cauldron that the palm-leaf manuscript also mentioned?" Reeya asked softly, talking mostly to herself.

"Along with the zinc that came from these mines, wootz was the other metal that was most sought after. Zinc from these mines was used to produce brass worldwide. Well, at least in the known world at the time. Wootz, on the other hand, was mostly used to make swords and knives. Shiploads of these metals were exported along well-established trading routes," Reeya said, giving Kabir a quick summary.

"I knew that the Indian subcontinent was a very prosperous region with famed riches. Columbus wouldn't have set sail to look for India if it were not so," ECG mused. "But I have only heard about spices and textiles. Even though I work here, I did not give it a thought in the broader context. This is the first time I've learnt what else contributed to this prosperity."

"It still doesn't tell us what exactly Myra is after," Kabir said, steering the discussion back to the case. "I'm feeling more confident, though, that we are headed in the right direction. But why that picture of the pot?" Kabir said, pointing to the carving of the cauldron that now seemed relevant to the story of wootz. "It doesn't seem improbable that they made a container in steel. But what was so unique about it that they carved its image on the stone?"

"Maybe it was the first time that humans used a steel container to cook for a big party," he joked with a faint smile. "Is there a recipe somewhere in Brahmi script? I wonder if it is good enough to die for… and kill for!"

"It talks about a soup so hot that only the gods could handle the heat. It says the soup stayed hot and kept getting hotter on its own. And melted even the pot over time. I cannot really be sure what they are saying, though, as some characters are missing. I will need more time and equipment to decipher it in detail."

"So, we have a piece of wootz, let's call it ancient steel. And we have a soup so hot that only the gods could handle it. And it is something that was to be kept hidden from the world, until the world was ready for it. I am not sure I understand the significance of it," Kabir was literally scratching his head.

"Does it say anything else? Does it say how they heated the soup?" Kabir asked. Reeya didn't have the answer as she had translated everything she could.

"Maybe that's the mystery. A pot that heats up the soup by itself," Reeya offered. "It clearly says the soup kept getting hotter, but does not mention how."

"Maybe the magic was in the combination of the soup and the pot?" ECG chimed in. "We have not been able to unearth much of what the ancient civilisations knew. But we do know they were well-versed in alchemy. For example, they were using zinc powder to cure certain skin ailments. Almost like it's used for diaper rash today."

It was all conjecture, but the mysterious inscription had got them thinking. Even though Reeya could read the script it was written in, she was unable to conclusively decipher the entire piece.

"Let's go with the working theory that the ancients had possibly found a process to heat a liquid to extremely high temperatures," Kabir said thoughtfully. His instinct said they needed an expert to throw more light on the ancient mystery.

"Is there anything else we need from here?" Kabir asked as he saw Reeya taking photos of the writing and sketches on the wall.

Reeya was taking pictures on her smartphone when she saw some rubble in the corner of the room. Shining her torchlight on the pile, she saw something that looked like an earthen tablet. Clearing out the rubble, she realised it was engraved, and it started with the short and long dashes she had seen before.

"Kabir, help me pull this out!" Reeya said excitedly.

Kabir walked carefully along the stone pathway, avoiding the lamp stands that protruded from the channel. He reached the rubble where Reeya was holding on to the stone engraving. Holding it from the top, Kabir pulled it out and carried it back to the altar. Resting it against the wall, he cleaned it with his hands, using the little water in the channel. Reeya stood there shining her torch, impatient to read what the text said.

But the engraved tablet was not complete. The first thought that flashed into their minds was that it was the other half of the tablet! It was what Myra was looking for. *But how had it gotten here?*

"We are in the right place," concluded Reeya as Kabir nodded. ECG was puzzled by their body language that clearly indicated they knew something that he didn't.

"We need to carry this with us," Kabir announced.

"But how will we find Myra and the other half?"

"Let's cross that bridge when we get to it," Kabir said, more interested in knowing what the part tablet said.

Even he could hear the urgency in his voice. He was chafing to go back up and connect with Nair, the one person he could implicitly trust.

Sensing his impatience, Reeya put her hand on his arm as she moved closer to read the script on the tablet. Her gentle touch calmed Kabir's anxiety.

Reeya read out what she could from the tablet…

"… *guardians who knew of this ancient place made that hole deeper than the hill itself. The sand and salt covered the ancient centre of the world. The dig took place for seven days and seven nights. It was done four* dhanus *away from one edge of the gate, which is three* dhanus *wide. It was five* dhanus *from the other edge of the gate.*"

"There was an ancient centre of the world?" Kabir said in surprise.

"Yes, the Indus Valley civilisation was essentially the first commercial centre of the world. It enjoyed a very exalted place in the limited world order at the time. It was a contemporary of the Egyptian and Mesopotamian civilisations and several times larger than both combined,[125]" Reeya explained.

"Wow!" Kabir exclaimed, trying to imagine the world 5000 years ago. But this was not the time or place to go off into a daydream about the ancient past.

"While there are several contenders in that period, such as Harappa, Mohenjo-Daro, Rakhigarhi, and many other major sites, 'covered by sand and salt', narrows down the scope considerably. The original Ahar folks living here were contemporaries of the ancient cities of Lothal and Dholavira.[126] I cannot pinpoint a particular location, but it has to be the Kutch region in Gujarat," Reeya said, sounding confident about her deduction, "but…"

'But what? Kabir prompted.

"Dholavira and Lothal were large cities, while Ahar was their rural counterpart. They were all quite advanced for 3500 BCE or even earlier when they existed.[127] They made some refined pottery, and their beads were highly sought after in the ancient world. However, there is absolutely no connection with wootz," she explained. "It is unlikely that they produced refined iron by the time they dispersed to other locations. And, by our estimates, Lothal and Dholavira would have been engulfed by the jungle and turned into mounds by about 1500 BCE[128]. But the script here, and the wootz, came much later."

"Even if that was the case, the people living here would have known about the ancient cities of Lothal and Dholavira, right?" Kabir said, trying to figure things out.

"Conventional history puts the discovery of wootz or zinc mining at Zawar much after the decline of Indus Valley towns such as Lothal and Dholavira. The first-known reference to steel outside of South India appears around the 5th century BCE,[129] when swords made of this material were gifted to the King of Persia.[130] The metal from the Chera kingdom of South India was also initially known as iron from Seres, as the Greeks called the Cheras, before being known as Seric steel[131]. There was a 1000-year gap between the last-known Dholavira population and the first-known ancient steel," Reeya concluded.

"The people who were living here and producing zinc were contemporaries of those making wootz in the south of India. Neither culture knew about any of the locations of the Indus civilisation. But somehow, a small group of alchemists seemed to have known about these cities," Kabir said, trying to sum up what he had understood. "They experimented with this steel pot and then had to find a place to hide it? And chose to hide it in one of the Indus Valley cities? Did I get that correct?"

"Yes. Nothing I know would indicate that those who lived here had any knowledge of the Indus cities. But I suppose what you are saying is possible," Reeya agreed. "Based on the inscription, I'd say they hid the pot in Lothal or Dholavira. Lothal was a centre of commerce and fashion, while Dholavira was the larger centre, likely administrative. Those are the two main cities we know of from the Indus civilisation that are near sand and salt. While there are several other civilisation centres in the area, like Ahar or Balathal, they were not covered by sand or salt."

It was dark by the time they came out of the mines, carrying the broken tablet with them. ECG protested feebly that they were not allowed to carry any artefacts from the site, but Kabir paid no heed.

The guard at the entrance of the mine was gone. Kabir found it disconcerting. He looked around to check for any signs of danger.

"Where is the guard?" he asked ECG, who was switching off the lights of the shaft.

"His shift must be over, and he must have gone home. We don't have a night guard. I'll have to finish up here now that he is gone," ECG answered casually as he continued closing up.

Trained to anticipate danger, Kabir was not reassured by ECG's explanation. He kept his eyes peeled for anything unusual as they walked back. Knowing how desperately someone wanted the broken tablet, he felt they were in serious danger now that they were in possession of it. His gut feeling was that the mercenaries already knew which city the cauldron was buried in based on the other half of the tablet that they held. They only needed Reeya and Kabir's half for the precise location of where to dig.

Sensing his unease, Reeya comforted him, "We'll be ok." Kabir nodded, and, strangely, her words did have a calming effect.

Reaching the dark and desolate parking lot in front of the office building, Kabir and Reeya bid ECG goodbye, thanking him for his help.

Kabir wrapped the tablet carefully in layers of tissue paper—the only covering he could find. He hoped it would be adequate to protect the relic. Placing it securely in the back, he jumped into the driver's seat and got the car moving before he spoke.

"Where to now?" he asked, still vigilant about a sudden interception or a shadowy figure emerging.

"To Lothal. I think," Reeya added to express her tentativeness. "Both Lothal and Dholavira were large urban sites that would have been at least partly covered by sand and salt. Lothal, just because it is closer," Reeya explained.

Kabir was glad to have clear direction on where to head next. They had almost reached the point on the highway where they had to decide which way to turn.

"Lothal it is," concurred Kabir energetically, looking at a set of headlights in the rear-view mirror, that had been keeping a distance but seemed to be headed in the same direction.

14
New Delhi

THE STATE-OF-THE-ART CONFERENCE ROOM WAS LARGE, WITH a table that could easily seat sixteen people. The large panels on one wall highlighted situations threatening humanity across the globe. The maps and charts were a handy reference tool to help the three men seated at the table make decisions for neutralising the threats.

Oddly, none of the three was paying attention to the colourful displays on the wall. They were in a huddle, conversing seriously in low voices even though there was no need to whisper in the soundproof room that had been swept for bugs.

The steel and glass building that housed the room was well guarded against both physical and cyber threats. No electronic equipment could be brought into the building without the security's knowledge, and every communication device in the facility was tracked. A fortress of sorts, the conference room was a sanctuary within the fortress.

While it was impossible to sneak in a listening device, there was no restriction on the delicious food the three men were enjoying. They spoke intermittently between succulent bites of the *kathi* rolls that had just been delivered. The small pieces of goat meat, marinated in a sauce made using a three-generation-old recipe, and rolled up in thin *roomali rotis* were gaining favour in the office at lunchtime.

"These *kathi* rolls are delicious," declared the man in the middle as he took another large bite from his package.

The strong, muscular physique he must have had in his younger days had aged well. The head of the organisation, who was generally referred to as Chief or Mr Singh, looked like someone it wouldn't be prudent to cross. Perhaps it was his gleaming deep-set eyes and large bushy eyebrows that gave him a look of razor-sharp intelligence.

The youngest of the three, generally referred to by his first name, Ritvik, nodded in agreement. His easy-going appearance disguised the enormity of the responsibility placed on him as the head of communications. He was approachable and well-liked. And he had been responsible for assembling state-of-the-art equipment and appointing the personnel that manned it. A significant amount of sensitive information flowed from his department and had never been known to be compromised. He had managed to successfully install safeguards at every step of the flow that ensured smooth passage of information without in any way compromising its confidentiality.

"I wish we were eating in happier circumstances," Ritvik said, proceeding to take another bite.

"Who else knew about this?" Nair demanded, knowing he deserved answers as the deputy chief. Nair had called the meeting with the chief to convince him that Kabir could not be the murderer. Singh, in turn, had asked Ritvik to join the meeting.

"I am sure there is a leak in the department somewhere," Nair expressed his concern.

"The chief had the same concern when I presented the evidence," Ritvik said with a nod of acknowledgement. "And we've started looking for a mole."

"In the meantime, we need to ask Kabir to come in. Let's not allow our emotions to cloud our judgement." Singh was looking at his deputy as he spoke, clearly understanding the special relationship Nair had with Kabir.

"Kabir did not know of the professor's existence when he was shot," protested Nair. "And what about Myra and her gang flying to Bhopal just as Kabir and Reeya landed there? How would Kabir have given them an indication even if he was somehow involved?"

Singh nodded sympathetically and explained, "We are not saying that he is part of this. There is always the possibility that there is a mole in this building. But what if there isn't? Kabir could have committed the crimes you mention."

"Myra shot at him. Why would she do that if he was involved with them?" said Nair in a respectful yet firm tone.

"But she missed," pointed out Ritvik. "We are still compiling the lists as requested by the Chief of anyone who knew of Kabir's whereabouts. And that would include the three of us," Ritvik said, defending the impartiality of his investigation.

"Do that," affirmed the deputy with a nod. "And since we track all calls in and out of this building, the person would have had to leave the building to pass the information in person or even call someone."

"I assume you already have a list of those who left the building before Myra knew of Kabir's location?" Nair said, looking at Ritvik questioningly.

"Here is the list of those who were out or went out that day. Many go out during lunch, so it is a rather long list." Having hand-picked his people, Ritvik was insistent on proving that the mole wasn't on his team. "But we will find the rat, if we indeed have one."

"Don't disregard any evidence that comes along," the chief told them both firmly. He realised that each one was trying to protect the members of his team. He added ominously, "But what about those not in this building?" Both men knew what the Chief was alluding to.

"Besides us, only key members of the home ministry and the chief minister are involved," Ritvik said, adding as an afterthought, "And the professor, of course. But since neither the chief minister nor the home ministry is operationally involved, I did not include them in the list of suspects.

"Hmmm..." Singh agreed. Satisfied that the two had nothing more to add, he turned to Nair. "Do we know more about who is funding the mercenaries?"

"We do have information that Ezio may be behind this," Nair responded and waited for Singh to assimilate his thoughts.

"How would a history professor be a threat to Ezio and his various legal and illegal businesses?" Singh said after a pause.

As the Chief had expected, Nair shook his head and replied, "We don't know yet."

They obviously didn't have enough evidence yet to request help from Interpol for questioning Ezio. The three men were familiar with Ezio's empire and the intricacies of how his human trafficking and drugs, and arms dealing were piggybacking on his known energy and shipping businesses. However, they could not see any connection between the professor and Ezio's legal and illegal business empire.

What could the professor possibly have unearthed that would make Ezio feel threatened? Or perhaps it was something that was deeply desired by him?

15
Abu Road

Day 3 | 2100 hrs

KABIR HAD BEEN DRIVING SOUTHWARDS ON THE HIGHWAY FOR a few minutes while keeping an eye on the headlights in his rear-view mirror. He had not mentioned the car to Reeya, so as not to worry her.

He saw a service road coming up and decided to take that exit unexpectedly.

"Hang tight!" Kabir said, almost simultaneously as he made the manoeuvre, without giving Reeya any time to react. He veered the SUV abruptly off the highway.

Reeya steadied herself, looking at Kabir as she bounced in the car on the unpaved rural road. Realising something was wrong, she turned around to look behind them, with an unspoken question on her lips.

"Stay low," he instructed Reeya as he took another turn to get further away from the highway. He turned off the SUV's headlights and continued to drive while observing the car which was behind them.

He let out a sigh of relief when he saw the headlights continue southwards. He proceeded back onto the highway, only to find the car had pulled over to one side of the highway.

"I think that car is following us," Kabir said, gesturing with his head to the parked car. "I'm going to find out what the problem is." Ignoring Reeya's protests, Kabir continued straight ahead towards the vehicle.

He stopped a little behind the car. He had left his headlights on and was sure that the driver would be able to see their SUV in the rearview mirror.

"Keep your head down," instructed Kabir while expertly releasing the safety catch on his handgun.

He stepped out of the vehicle and slipped into the shadows of the large shrubs that grew on the side of the highway. He quickly moved towards the passenger side of the stopped car and raised his gun towards the driver.

"ICU?" Kabir exclaimed, trying to recall his name.

"ECG," corrected a faltering voice, partly raising his hands as he saw the gun in Kabir's hand.

"Why were you following us?" Kabir asked with a confused look.

"Professor Khosla rang just as you left, sounding very shaky as he told me that your life was in danger. He asked me to follow you, but to keep a safe distance and to call the cops in case you were attacked," ECG said, lowering his hands as Kabir tucked the gun behind his back.

"What else did he say?" Kabir asked more firmly than he had intended.

"Nothing," ECG replied. "Just to keep him updated on where you went."

"And did you do that?" Kabir continued, though without the angry edge to his voice.

"Yes, I did tell him when you got on the highway, going south." ECG was perplexed at Kabir's demeanour. He didn't seem worried at being told that his life was in danger, though seeing Kabir carrying a handgun shook him.

"Who are you?" ECG finally mustered the courage to ask.

"Don't worry about that. Yes, there are people trying to harm us, but you should go back home. Tell Professor Khosla that you lost us on the highway. And say nothing else. That will keep you safe as well. Understood?" Kabir said compellingly.

He signalled to ECG to head back. And ECG was all too eager to comply. He made a U-turn and raced down the road, even before Kabir could walk back to the SUV.

Getting back into the driver's seat, Kabir narrated what had happened to Reeya and how he had sent ECG back.

"I don't see any reason why Professor Khosla would ask ECG to keep an eye on us unless he was made to do it under duress. We should remain vigilant," said Kabir worriedly. "It will take a few hours to get to Ahmedabad. We may run into either the police or Myra and her crew."

A few hundred kilometres to the north, Professor Khosla was a nervous wreck. He took the phone as ECG called. Sitting between two heavily armed men in the back of a large SUV, Professor Khosla summoned every ounce of remaining courage to keep the tremble from his voice.

"They are headed south from Zawar. Towards Ahmedabad. My man lost them on the highway," Professor Khosla said in a pleading tone.

The SUV slowed to a crawl, and the armed man to his left moved, just enough, to allow Professor Khosla to be pushed out of the vehicle. The door was shut, and the large SUV continued south on the highway, hoping to catch up with Kabir.

Despite having fallen from the vehicle, the professor was thanking the heavens for sparing his life. With good reason. He had not expected to survive the evening.

It had all started with a delivery person knocking at his door.

"There is a parcel for Mr Kabir," the delivery boy said.

"He's already left. I don't think he is coming back," Professor Khosla had opened the door and instinctively responded. "Can it be returned to the sender?"

He realised his mistake almost immediately as two others emerged from behind the boy and forced the door open with a gun pointing at him.

"But I don't know where he went," shuddered Professor Khosla without needing to be prompted.

"Calm down. We are not here for you. We just want to know what you told them and where they went," Myra's voice was slow and purposeful as she continued to toy with her gun absent-mindedly. "I am sure you can help.

"Did you drop him anywhere? I will treat you with respect, but please assume I can tell the difference between the truth and a lie. And I'd find it very disrespectful if you lied to me." There was no need to put the implicit threat into words.

"I dropped him off in the market. I swear I don't know where he went after that." The professor proceeded to ramble on about how Kabir and Reeya had shown up in the morning. He tried omitting the part about Zawar, but giving in to fear, he blurted it out.

"He was to meet someone at Zawar in the evening. He'd have left Zawar by now, but I can find him. Please don't kill me," Professor Khosla pleaded.

Like taking candy from a baby, Myra thought. She was pleased with herself for having perfected the art of instilling fear in the hearts of grown men. Her lucky guess of looking up a prominent archaeologist in the area had worked out and led her to Professor Khosla's door.

"Call your man and find out where he is," Myra had instructed the professor.

Professor Khosla, still nervous and trembling with fear, did his best to speak to ECG in a normal voice. ECG told the professor about the evening and that Kabir and Reeya had left, but he didn't know where they were headed.

"Have him follow them," whispered Myra in the professor's ear, as she pointed her gun at him, gesturing him to the door. "And you are coming with us."

Having been jettisoned out of the car, still in his pyjamas, Professor Khosla was thankful just to be alive. He slowly walked back home and said a grateful prayer when he reached home in one piece.

Kabir ran the various scenarios across his mind as he continued driving. He was convinced that Myra would not be far behind, and the only way to lose her would be to enter a large city. He was not sure if the police agencies were being misinformed by her organisation, but he had to assume the worst.

"Can you tone down the thinking? It is so loud," Reeya said with a giggle.

"Was it that obvious?" Kabir joined in the laughter and proceeded to lay out his assumptions to Reeya.

"It seems to me we should make a U-turn and head back to where we can fork off to Dholavira," Reeya suggested.

"Myra would have picked up the information that ECG had and would assume that we are going south towards Lothal. What if we turned back and then connected to the highway to Dholavira?" she explained her reasoning. "She would also have figured that we have the other half of the broken tablet."

Kabir nodded as he agreed with Reeya's assessment. It was a much longer route, but Kabir liked the idea. Assuming Myra was indeed feeding information to the law enforcement authorities, the Gujarat police would be on the lookout for them. Going to Dholavira would entail travelling through Rajasthan for much longer. And he was quite confident that the Rajasthan police hadn't been alerted.

"What are the odds that Lothal is where the artefact is hidden?" Kabir said.

"Lothal was a bustling metropolis. It was a town thriving on business, local and global[132]. It was the only town with a man-made harbour that sheltered seafaring ships[133]. It's where you'd shop for branded cotton garments at that time. It also had large warehouses where these ships could unload their cargo[134]."

"By contrast," Reeya continued to paint a picture that was simple yet historically accurate. "Dholavira was a much larger town. It could possibly have been the centre of government and learning. It certainly was very well-planned[135]. Their ability to harvest water was very sophisticated. From collecting rainwater to channelling it and keeping it safe from contamination[136]. They even had catchments so debris could be safely handled and did not impede the flow[137]. Constructing and managing all these systems, perhaps, was no less sophisticated than the erection of pyramids happening around the same time," Reeya said, unable to mask the admiration in her voice.

"The probability of it being in either location is about the same. We were headed to Lothal mostly because it was closer. We should change direction and head to Dholavira—and as I think about it, Dholavira being an Island at that time, may have been a better hiding place. Though I can't be sure." Reeya said, giving the assessment that Kabir was looking for.

Kabir saw an exit designed specifically for taking a U-turn. "So Dholavira it is," Kabir said as he veered towards the U-turn.

Reeya nodded in agreement as they headed back north. The highway was rather desolate. Reeya looked at Kabir's face in the dim light that the instrument panel provided. She felt butterflies in her stomach as she saw that determined, chiselled jaw.

"Kabir, let me drive. You take a nap," Reeya volunteered. "We can then switch again, so we can both get some rest."

Kabir knew that lack of rest and exhaustion would be his biggest enemy if things went on for much longer. They needed to figure out a way to rest and eat—to stay charged.

He nodded in agreement. "I'll stop at the next *dhaba* and we can get something for us to eat. You can drive from there."

Reeya had been craving for some *dhaba* food since they first got onto the highway. But there had been no time to stop anywhere. Time was still against them, but they did need to eat.

"I used to love *dhaba* food as a child," Reeya said absent-mindedly. Kabir's grim expression gave way to a smile. He found her musings rather endearing. "There was this stretch of six *dhabas*, all within a kilometre of each other, and each competing to make the best *daal* and chicken. The trucks and cabs would line up for their food. My dad would sometimes take my mom and me there and let me pick the *dhaba*. I had my favourites, and they'd change by the season. I liked *Bittoo Da Dhaba* for their chicken. And *Happy Da Dhaba* had this mind-blowing *daal*. I can taste it even now. I have tried to find the same flavour, but none came close."

Then she turned to Kabir and laughed, "Do you think it was because I was a really hungry kid that I found the taste simply divine?"

Kabir just smiled and said, "Possibly. But you must be just as hungry now. Let's find out if hunger alone can make you discover the same divine taste at this *dhaba* too."

Kabir was glad Reeya had this ability to forget their troubles and channel the conversation into unrelated subjects. It helped him relax for a while, too, forgetting that they were being chased by criminals and police alike and their lives were in serious danger.

"There is a *dhaba* just ahead. Let's stop there. They have scrumptious Rajasthani cuisine." Kabir had some knowledge of the area.

The service lane and highway were not separated by much more than a patch of wild grass and tropical shrubs. The unpaved patch of land that served as a makeshift parking lot was well-lit with overhead lights. Kabir parked closer to the *dhaba* and proceeded to find a table.

He scouted the place and settled for a table that was closer to the rear entrance of the *dhaba*. He saw the owner sitting near the entrance, collecting the payments as the patrons exited the establishment. He was middle-aged and seemed warm and cordial.

As they sat at a table, a young boy came up and rattled off the menu items at an amazing speed, and then waited for a response. Kabir and Reeya both knew what they wanted and barely heard what the boy said. After ordering, they both settled into their cane armchairs and looked at the eclectic décor of the place.

Reeya seemed excited, in anticipation of the fresh, hot Rajasthani *rotlas*, accompanied by the freshly prepared vegetables and curries. They were both very hungry and devoured the food as quickly as it was served. They stayed just long enough to finish and were quickly on their way again.

Reeya was at the wheel, and Kabir reclined the passenger seat as far as he could. Reeya encouraged him not to worry about the drive and just take a nap.

"I'll be ok. If I see any sign of danger, I'll wake you up," Reeya assured Kabir.

Kabir closed his eyes and drifted off as the Reeya smoothly sped along the highway. It was going to be a long, nine-hour drive.

16
Dholavira

It was early morning with the rising sun barely starting to illuminate the sky. Reeya and Kabir had been on the road for several hours now, taking turns to drive and catching up on sleep.

Reeya, who was now fully awake, was going over every word of the tablet again and again. She was making notes from the pictures she had taken in the Udayagiri caves with her smartphone.

"Something is wrong," Kabir said to Reeya. She looked up from the items that formed the puzzle she was trying to solve. Looking through the windshield, she could not see what had prompted Kabir to that conclusion.

Noticing her puzzled expression, Kabir continued, "It is too quiet. It almost feels like we are being left alone on purpose. There is just one way in or out of Dholavira by road. If there is going to be an ambush, this would be the logical place. I don't see any signs of one, though."

Kabir could see the only causeway leading to Khadir Island, where Dholavira is located, stretching out in front of him for several kilometres. It also served as a dam, with the rainwater accumulating on its northern side. When the flood gates were left open, the water would cross over to the southern side and eventually flow into the ocean.

The island was surrounded by a water body. It would fill up with rainwater in the monsoons, but come summer, all that remained was water saturated with salt[138]. Reeya was looking forward to seeing the ruins and showing Kabir the advanced nature of the civilisation and the city that once existed there. She wanted to share the many mysteries that still surrounded it. With no known predators, man or animal, the first mystery was why a city already on an island had been fortified.

Kabir continued driving on the narrow causeway leading to the island.

"I'd have enjoyed showing you the ruins at leisure under different circumstances," Reeya said regretfully as they drove over the causeway.

With a smile, Kabir inquired, "What kind of circumstances would you have preferred?" He felt a sense of comfort travelling with Reeya and could sense the attraction between them growing.

Reeya had struggled with her feelings for Kabir and could only hope they were not on the rebound. His question brought up the scenario she had visualised, and she deflected it with a grin, "Like a regular tourist, you know, just sightseeing." Her voice trailed off, and she lowered her gaze.

They were approaching the end of the causeway, and lush green grassland and short acacia trees lay all around. These trees were not indigenous to the region and were spray-planted in the region during the 1970s. The humidity they created made for an eerie, low layer of mist that drifted through the pale dawn light.

At a distance, Kabir could see a herd of cows occupying the road, as though it were quite the place to be for a morning walk. Not an uncommon sight at this early hour as they move to fresher pastures. Kabir slowed as he rolled down the window. He yelled at the cowherd to move the cows to the side and let him pass, but in vain.

Kabir slowly inched along behind the cows, trying to persuade the cowherd, and that's when he saw it. A black SUV was right in the middle of the cows, facing him menacingly. He stopped when he saw Myra through the windshield, looking at him casually, without a care in the world.

It was unlike Myra to position herself more like a prey than a predator. If she had intended to kill him, she would have been perched on one of the hills that lined the causeway.

Ignoring the cows, Myra stepped out of the vehicle. The cows continued to slowly amble by, oblivious of any obstruction in their movement. Kabir reciprocated the move and exited his own vehicle. Kabir signalled to Reeya to stay calm and remain inside the vehicle. "It is going to be ok," he reassured her.

Myra was composed and seemed to have anticipated him reaching for the gun he had tucked behind his back as he got out and moved slowly towards her.

"Put that gun away," Myra instructed Kabir, displaying her empty hands, to demand the same courtesy. "I could have killed you several times over as you crossed the causeway. If I had wanted."

Kabir was still clutching his gun with his hand behind his back, not sure what to make of the situation. He scanned the surroundings for Myra's team but couldn't see anyone else.

"There is one up there," Myra said, gesturing at a sniper perched atop a hill. "And the others are guarding the gates of Dholavira."

Inside their SUV, Reeya was tightly clutching the half of the tablet they had found in the Zawar mines. She concluded that she was not safe from a bullet even if she stayed inside the car. She wrapped the tablet and placed it on the floor of her seat, knowing fully well that attempts at hiding it were futile. She proceeded to slowly get out and stand with Kabir.

Kabir could see that Myra had the advantage over them with a sniper who had him and Reeya in his telescopic viewfinder. He could also see that Myra was raising her hands as if in surrender, to convey that she meant no harm.

"I have a simple proposal for you." Myra's tone was melodramatic, reminding Kabir of the many movie villains he had seen. "You know that neither of us can find the cauldron without the other half of the tablet. I could have killed you to get the other half. I can, in fact, kill you now. But I want to explain something first. I am sure you have not figured out what you are looking for. I know, and I assure you that you can have it. I have no interest in it," Myra proclaimed dryly. "I just want to get Ezio here so I can kill him, and I need your word that you will not interfere.

"I don't see it as a bad option for you. And if you feel you don't want to accept it, I can kill you now," Myra reiterated, with a smile that said she knew she held all the cards.

"But why do you want to kill Ezio?" Kabir was puzzled by Myra's demands.

"I have my reasons. I know you to be a man of your word. If you help me, I can tell you what Ezio is after, and why." Myra knew this was a generous offer and fully expected Kabir to take it.

Kabir found the interaction surreal. He did not want to let the professor's killer get away with it. He also realised that he wasn't really being given an option.

"If I help you, you'll have to let us go." Kabir sought to get some additional advantage. "And I'll also want the name of the mole."

Myra laughed and replied, "I have no interest in hurting you or Reeya. As for the mole, I don't know who it is, but I can help you reach him." Myra's expression hardened. Kabir could see the pain and hatred. "He will be useless once I kill Ezio.

"Ezio killed Novak, my boyfriend." Through a clenched jaw, Myra announced, "He must pay for what he did. He did not know that Novak and I were together. We were going to get married. We were looking to get out of this life of servitude to Ezio," Myra said with tears filling her fierce eyes.

Kabir knew how Myra must feel. If he could get his hands on Vani's killer, he knew he would avenge her death above all else. But that didn't discount the fact that Myra had killed the professor.

"I'm sorry to hear that," Kabir said sympathetically. "But why did you kill the professor?"

"My sniper did kill the guard, but the Professor's death was unfortunate. He had stumbled on something that could be very damaging to Ezio." Myra paused and realised she'd need to explain further. "As you know, we use uranium and plutonium in our nuclear reactors today. Have you ever paused to think why, or if there are any non-explosive alternatives available?"

Kabir considered answering the question using the rudimentary knowledge he had, but took the easier course of throwing it back to Myra, "Tell me."

Myra took a deep breath as she started to explain the details of how the professor had stumbled upon a virtually unlimited green energy source that threatened Ezio's empire.

"I have heard about projects of that nature," confessed Kabir. "Though, I don't know if much has come out of them yet. I know that the government is now spending a lot more on this research path." Kabir could see where Myra was going with the theory, but was sceptical of her objective. "Are you saying that they had figured out this process in ancient India?"

Shaking her head, Myra spoke, "No, no, that is not what I'm implying. What we know so far is inconclusive. But if we can find the wootz container that was used to try to contain the reaction, it would change the dynamics significantly."

"How so?" Kabir asked, trying to make sense of it.

"Well, Ezio is afraid that having proof that such a project was done in ancient India will galvanise the government and people to accelerate the development significantly. And that if this goes mainstream faster than expected, it will be the death of his oil network empire. He has also invested billions into competing energy sources, including nuclear fusion, which is still trillions of dollars away from being commercially viable. His investments are at risk."

"But how can Ezio stop this from happening?" Kabir was curious. "Won't it happen eventually?"

"Yes, it will happen eventually. The crux is the pace of development. India has the skill and resources, but knowing it was done here earlier may accelerate commercialisation significantly," Myra explained.

"This could solve the world's energy problem. And to think that the ancients may already have stumbled on and worked in this direction many millennia ago," Kabir exclaimed in wonder.

"We still need to find the wootz vessel to prove anything, though," Reeya said, wanting to be the one to discover the world-changing artefact.

"There is more," Myra added, carefully selecting her words. "Ezio is a driven personality, to put it mildly. He follows a cult that has, over the years, provided him with valuable information. He has now been led to believe that in ancient times, the cult had discovered the power of the cauldron, and he now shoulders the sacred responsibility to retrieve it. It has made him obsessive in his quest, also more dangerous. So first, we need to make sure that Ezio is coming to retrieve it." Myra seemed to have a plan in mind. "It's time you called the deputy chief."

"That's a tall ask. Let's say I trust you. But I still need to know what you have in mind," Kabir said curiously.

"Hand your gun over and I'll tell you in detail," Myra replied in a serious tone. "We will have to trust each other for this to work," she added as Kabir nodded and pulled the gun from behind his back to hand it over.

"Slowly!" Myra instructed as she reached out to take the gun from Kabir. She instructed Kabir to turn around as she frisked him to ensure he wasn't carrying any other weapons.

"How did you know that we'd come to Dholavira?"

"It was spelt out on the tablet fragment we picked up from Giriyak. So, we knew that sooner or later you'd find your way here. And we will need both halves to find the precise location of the artefact," she said with a confident smile. She picked up a branch off the ground and started to sketch on the dirt as she explained her plan in detail.

Walking to his SUV, Kabir reached for the bag that Raghvendra had packed and took out the burner phone. He dialled the number he had memorised and used several times earlier.

"Sir," Kabir said without giving his name. "We have a lead."

"Speak freely. This phone is not being tracked. I suspected you'd be calling on Vani's old number," Nair reassured

Kabir. Kabir was glad he had given Vani's broken phone to Nair, knowing that he'd get it repaired for the photos that it contained.

Kabir was relieved as he proceeded to explain the recent developments and Myra's plan. "This should flush out the mole as well."

The plan was underway.

17

Khadir Island

THE THREE MEN WERE HUDDLED IN THE NIA OFFICE AS NAIR informed the other two about the call he had received from Kabir.

"He believes Ezio is behind the mercenaries. That is in line with what we already know," Nair informed the chief and Ritvik, who were listening intently.

"Kabir has provided us with a short list of possible locations that Myra could be headed. He believes that she may already have the information for the last mile. We will need to move quickly to secure all the locations," Nair's tone was urgent.

"He believes she may be looking for a vessel made of ancient steel—known as wootz—that may have been used to ensure non-explosive nuclear fission." Nair paused, glancing at the other two for their reaction.

"Kabir has provided us with four possible locations, but he feels that Myra is most likely heading to Dholavira. I suggest we send one team to each location," Nair laid out the plan. "We may have only a few hours before she reaches the location, so we should set things in motion immediately."

"Dr Momita Harinath is on the line with the information you had requested urgently," the intercom came to life, interrupting Nair.

"Put her through," he said curtly.

"Dr Harinath is the thorium expert at the Department of Atomic Energy. I had left a detailed message for her so she could provide an input on the threat assessment," Nair explained to the others.

"What have you found, Dr Harinath? What kind of dangers are we talking about here?" Nair said to turn on the physical switch for the video system to be activated in the secure meeting room.

"Good morning, gentlemen," Dr Harinath said with a smile, not aware of the tense mood in the room. "Firstly, let me put you gentlemen at ease. We are not facing any significant danger or destruction here—there will be no nuclear explosion or any such catastrophe."

Dr Harinath's smile lightened the mood in the room. It also left the three men in the room confused. How was it that a nuclear device posed no danger?

"We are aware of the rumours of an ancient device that was capable of producing thermal energy through nuclear reaction. But I can assure you that we have never found anything that can substantiate such rumours," Dr Harinath paused, and sensing that the men in the room were still equating nuclear with explosion, continued to address their immediate fears,

"More importantly, when we think of nuclear reactions, we think explosions. It need not be so."

"You mean you can have a nuclear reaction without an explosion or a danger of an explosion? Isn't the whole point of a nuclear reaction to spawn a chain reaction that, if left unchecked, could cause a catastrophic explosion?" Nair sought clarification.

Dr Harinath sensed that some background information would help dispel that myth. "When nuclear energy was developed during World War II, it was aimed at creating a weapon. The subsequent development of nuclear power was based on improving these weapon systems. Typically, uranium or plutonium is used as fissile material. Billions were poured into the research, and all modern reactors were the result of technology thus developed." Dr Harinath paused before asking a question.

"Yes, the common perception equates nuclear with explosion. But what if the nuclear reaction were not always a violent explosion and could be done on a smaller and cheaper scale? It is believed that the thorium-based molten salt reactors, T-MSR for short, can achieve just that." Dr Harinath was now looking intently at the three in the room through the video link.

Seeing that her audience was somewhat sceptical, she continued, "There is a lot of misinformation that floats around on the subject, including possible by-products that could be dangerous. While a lot of it may be legitimate concerns that need to be addressed through proper research, there is also propaganda.

"Some believe that the military-industrial complex, which has invested billions into the existing nuclear technology over the years, has systematically put out propaganda against T-MSR. It stands to reason that bringing in a viable alternative may be opposed by those that stand to lose their current business," Dr Harinath said, to explain the relatively modest investments in research on the alternative.

"Momita *Ji*, what does this have to do with ancient Indian artefacts?" Nair interrupted her. He wanted Dr Harinath to come to the point quickly, so he could get his team over to Dholavira to help Kabir.

Ignoring the interruption, Dr Harinath continued, "India would have been the obvious place for research on T-MSR as it has more known natural thorium deposits than any other country[139]. And in all fairness, we are and have a good, long-term strategy.

"Think about it for a minute. Why would a country with little or no such deposits invest in making MSR-based thorium reactors if they don't have any thorium and will need to import it?" Dr Harinath posed a vital question and continued after a pause, "While we have always doubted that such an artefact existed, finding any proof that this was done, even if at a rudimentary scale, several millennia ago, would energise the proponents! It would effectively disarm any sceptics and enable the scientific community to accelerate the process."

Momita Harinath took a pause and sensed she needed to illustrate her point to bring the message home. "My father-in-law is a history buff, and he likes to use classic names for everyday objects. He had once called our steel pressure cooker a wootz pressure cooker. It got me curious, and I did some research on the material. I know it was mostly used to make swords and sharp weapons, but the process was adaptable and could be applied to make a container of sorts."

She continued after a pause, "Also, thorium is abundantly available in India and in the world, at about four times the amount of uranium, and more easily extracted[140]. It does need some extraction from the sands in which it is found, but the process is not complex, and let's go with the assumption that the ancients had figured it out. Finally, and it is unlikely, but let's just say that they even manage to start a reaction.

"All this may not amount to much from a scientific standpoint, but if this becomes known to the masses, it will energise them to move towards success. Just as the successful Chandrayan launch has made us bolder in our space initiative, this will propel us to invest heavily and lead in T-MSR technology. While India is already one of the four key drivers in this program[141], this will give an even bigger push. Success does beget success, it is said.

"With the people inspired by the speech from their president, everyone in the USA got behind the programme to send a man to the moon. In much the same way, this discovery could inspire us to make a viable T-MSR reactor, perhaps before the end of the decade. Clean air and abundant green energy will be well within our reach! And not just for us, but the entire world!" She looked exhilarated as if she had already realised the dream.

Chief Singh's shoulders straightened while Nair leaned in with widened eyes. Ritvik let out a *whoosh* sound of exhaled air. The enthusiasm and the magnitude of the find sank in.

"One of the key obstacles we face in generating a thorium-based MSR reaction is that we don't have a suitable material that can be used as a container in the reactor. The reaction occurs at very high temperatures, and the molten salts themselves are highly corrosive. Though the high temperature makes the reactor more efficient compared to what we have today[142], the available materials to contain the molten salt don't last very long in these conditions. Ideally, the material should be such that it can remain intact for years, if not decades, before needing to be replaced," Dr Harinath said, outlining the first problem.

The three in the room were nodding their heads, anticipating where the conversation was going.

Dr Harinath continued in her jubilant tone. "Keep in mind that some have called the ancient wootz makers' accidental nanotechnologists[143]. Many ancient civilisations made use of nanotechnologies, not just the Indians. For example, Mayan pottery displayed a stunning blue due to metal and oxide nanoparticles on the surface[144]. Some variants of wootz show the presence of carbon nanowires[145]. It is possible that some variant may have accidentally shown a significant resistance to deterioration during a T-MSR experiment.

"If such a sample could be found, it would certainly increase the political will to fund the research. And the best part is, we could accelerate the research and lead in this sphere.

Additionally, since T-MSR could operate at atmospheric pressure, it minimises the need for any containment system associated with high-pressure systems in a traditional reactor that could breach and send contaminants into the air[146]. This makes it safer in many regards and will also open the anti-nuclear lobby to hearing out the merits.

"Of course, nothing is absolute in science. But the thorium MSR reactions do not lend themselves to being easily turned into a destructive device. Thorium itself is fertile, but not fissile, so it cannot be directly used to make nuclear bombs. Even when made fissile, it does not easily decay into a plutonium or uranium isotope that is favoured to make such devices[147]. The common perception that 'nuclear' means 'explosive' can be changed. It breaks the link of associating the word 'nuclear' with 'destruction'." She paused and then emphasised, "because of their inherent safety and compact size, it is not inconceivable to locate them near the areas of high demand, such as cities[148]. Of course, much research still needs to be done before arriving at that point."

"But how about the radioactive waste that gets generated? Isn't that one of the key problems? And it can be a lot of waste; the United States had to turn a whole mountain, Yucca Mountain, into a waste disposal site. It has collected something like $25B in fees over the last several years from the nuclear-power producers." Nair asked.

"From studies done with LFTR, a type of MSR, we know that the waste profile is one of the most attractive features. It makes very little[149]. And mind you, it even consumes much less. Some studies suggest that only 3.2 kilos of thorium per day would need to be mined to produce the same amount of power that an LWR reactor produces, with 680 kilos of uranium mining needed per day.[150]" She concluded.

"Hmmm... Favourable costs, lesser waste, smaller components, higher efficiency[151], so why has the world not chased after it already? And it seems it does not spew out greenhouse gases into the atmosphere either," Singh said as he absorbed the information.

Dr Harinath was expecting the question. With a smile, she answered. "The same reason that makes it safe is the reason we never funded it! See, the first big boost of funding for nuclear science happened during the Manhattan Project, the making of the atomic bomb. Billions were spent to understand the nature and uses of uranium and plutonium as they were needed to make the bomb. During the Cold War, even more was spent to maintain deterrence status quo by producing ever more powerful bombs. Of course, in India, we have funded research for MSR, but there are many other competing priorities that reduce the allocation for faster productisation and deployment at scale.

"Thorium was sidelined as it could not be used to produce the uranium or plutonium that was needed for thermonuclear devices. And now it seems like good hope for the future. Yes, it is ironic, I know," The three men in the room were finally connecting the dots and understood the implications of the wootz cauldron.

"Dr Harinath, just for argument's sake, if we were to find this 'magical' material, how quickly can we develop a viable commercial thorium-MSR reactor?" Singh asked.

Dr Harinath considered the implications of such a material existing and answered, "Let me put it this way, there are those of us who feel we are still 20-30 years away from commercialisation. We still spend most of our research budget on uranium and plutonium-based reactors. They are considered tried and tested technology.

"And then, there are some of us who believe that we could have the first commercial T-MSR ready before the end of the decade if we could divert more funding towards it. It would still take many years to establish and put in place safety regulations[152] and a certification process that can be agreed on, possibly internationally. Proponents of so-called Gen III+ reactors would argue against the need. The bureaucracy alone is not an easy task, but the tailwind provided by such a discovery will likely prove the latter group correct," she said optimistically as Nair concluded the call with all three of them thanking her for her valuable insights.

"Even if the programme was accelerated by only 10 years, it would mean a significant disruption in Ezio's network. If there were proof this was done millennia ago, there would be no dearth of believers, and if I may add—investors," Singh stated. "Ezio will start losing customers right away."

"It would cost him billions," Nair agreed. "He may not be able to stop the eventual adoption of the technology, but I can see why he would want to ensure that it is not accelerated."

"But, why now?" Singh was still curious about the timing. "The technology is not a big secret. Anyone who would care to search can look it up on the Internet. What can have spooked Ezio now?"

It was obvious—stopping the archaeological find that could accelerate T-MSR commercialisation didn't seem enough to explain the zeal with which Ezio was chasing after the artefact. They exchanged glances, acknowledging that there could be more to it than just stopping the find.

"I'll get the teams going," said Nair as Mr Singh and Ritvik nodded. "It will take our teams some time to get to their locations. My team will take about three hours, including an hour's drive from Bhuj, the nearest airport."

Nair still enjoyed fieldwork more than his desk job. He felt good being close to the action. He quickly chose leaders for each location and separately briefed each. Finally, he called the team he would be leading directly.

The team was assembled in the situation room. The men were sitting in a row, with their camouflaged backpacks matching their uniform, neatly lined next to the door. Nair walked in and greeted each of the five members by name. He knew them well as each one was hand-picked for their special abilities, along with a background in close-range combat.

The small team meeting room had a large panel on the wall, showing the satellite image of Dholavira and the surrounding areas. One could see the small island surrounded by brackish water with a single road leading into it from the eastern side.

Whipping out the telescope-indicator, Nair proceeded to explain the situation and the access route to Dholavira. "We will have to land here. We will be met by a tactical support team to drive to Dholavira. We should arrive before Kabir, and hopefully before Myra, and cut them off at this point." The sole bridge to Dholavira was the only option for the purpose, and he concluded with the final instruction, “Gear up and out in three minutes.”

The teams had all started to board their respective vehicles. Nair and his team were the last to leave. They would be donning their guerrilla fatigues once airborne. The casual banter continued among the otherwise professional colleagues as the small bus with dark windows made its way to the airport.

They entered from the side entrance to the tarmac, to find several small planes lining the area. The NIA’s planes were mixed in with a few civilian ones and some odd military transport planes.

“I need all cell phones and communication devices in this basket.” This protocol was not invoked often, but Nair ensured it was complied with.

The deputy chief then signalled to the men and women on the team to follow him. A short walk later, they were standing in front of a US-2 amphibian. The team was silent except for exchanging some quick glances. The puzzled look was expected. Why take an amphibian if the plan was to land at a nearby airport? Obviously, there was an unannounced change in plan.

Once the team was buckled, the deputy chief proceeded to explain in more detail, “Your phones are on the flight to Kutch airport. There is good reason to believe that they will be tracked. We will be landing in the water next to Khadir Island. Get in your gear after take-off.”

Ezio had been waiting for this call.

"The deputy chief and his team are headed to Dholavira. They have just left and will be reaching in about three hours. So, you have that much time to retrieve what you need and clear out the place," the voice on the phone said before disconnecting.

A curved sneer appeared on Ezio's face. He had received the call from Myra confirming Dholavira as the location, and she had indicated that she had the precise location of the artefact.

Ezio had survived in this world by never trusting any one person. Getting confirmation from the mole made him trust Myra's information better. He had just under three hours. *It was tight, but would be enough*, Ezio thought. Besides, he was stationed nearby, not to leave things to chance. And in case needed, he was prepared with a small army.

Ezio felt in control. Things were moving as per plan. He picked up the phone and called Myra. There was no response, but he was not concerned. *I'll try again in a few minutes*, he thought to himself.

The manuscript seemed to be telling the truth, he thought. He admired the view of the large expanse of water with a thin, white foam-like layer covering the salty water. Far away in the distance, he could see the hill on the island.

The sun was rising above the island, and a silhouette of the ancient ruins was emerging. He took out his secure device and called Myra again. Still no answer. Ezio was starting to get concerned. It was not like Myra to lose communication. What could have happened?

The devices were equipped to use satellites if needed. So, it couldn't be something as mundane as a lack of signal. Not picking up once could simply mean being busy. Not picking up twice could indicate trouble. He called again. Hoping she'd pick up this time. And she did.

"Stop calling and send help! We are under attack!" The urgency in Myra's voice was very convincing. "I've located the spot marked X, and we are digging for the artefact. But Kabir has caught up and has the higher ground. Get your ass here now!"

"Everyone! Break time is over. Get into the boat now!" Ezio yelled at his men in guerrilla attire.

They had been waiting on the other side of the water with a specially equipped boat. It could slice through the thin layer of salt that formed on the water.

Ezio was confident that his little army carried enough firepower to deal with almost any situation Kabir could present. Nothing was going to stop him from witnessing history. And yet, he only wanted to be there to ensure that the discovered artefact would never see the light of day.

But something didn't add up, Ezio could feel it in his bones.

18

The Spot Marked X

As they heard her story, Reeya thought to herself, either Myra was a brilliant storyteller or her suffering was so intense that nothing but revenge could appease it. Kabir could relate to her feelings. It was apparent that she needed them, or else, Myra's sniper wouldn't have left them alive for so long.

Kabir and Reeya had agreed to work with Myra. It benefited them all. Kabir was not comfortable with letting Myra get away with murder, but what were their options? He tried to console himself with the thought that maybe someday there would be a full reckoning and the professor's death would get justice.

They had joined the broken tablets to make it whole. Now they knew exactly where to find the wootz cauldron. As Kabir predicted, the guard on duty was unaware of Kabir and Reeya being on the wanted list and graciously let them in thanks to their identity cards. They traversed the site through the early morning light.

"Do you realise that there was a civilisation that lived here at least 5500 years ago?" Reeya's passion for history evidently was stronger than her appreciation of the sticky situation they were in, or maybe it was just a coping mechanism.

Although Kabir too had grown enamoured of ancient history being around Reeya, Myra's team was not so interested. But Myra herself seemed to be paying attention; perhaps it was her heritage that gave her a regard for ancient history.

"That would be way before the Archaic period of Greek civilisation, which did not even start till about 800 BCE.[153]" It was evident that Myra was not completely clueless about the history of her civilisation.

"Yes, it would be," confirmed Reeya. "And that is the date we get from studying the newer earth strata of the city. It is quite possible that civilisation started in 3500 BCE or even earlier."

Reeya led the small contingent, with Kabir and Myra close behind. They went past the Eastern reservoir as they entered the compound. The three heavily armed mercenaries spread out a little to keep an eye on all sides. The arms they carried made Reeya feel uncomfortable.

As they walked past the reservoir on their left, they were confronted with a large stub of a retaining wall. This was again crafted with unfinished stones, with steps cut in between to allow them to climb over it and reach the large central plateau.

They continued to move diagonally towards the opening in the outer wall, which formed a corridor that was the entrance to the inner complex. The corridor was lined with highly polished circular granite column bases. Each of these circular

Figure 7: *Polished Stone Column base at Dholavira*

bases was set atop a similarly polished rectangular rock. Pieces of what would have been the column shaft lay broken nearby.

"Does this remind you of the ancient Greek temples?" enquired Reeya, glancing at Myra.

Myra nodded and gently touched the structures as she passed by them. "And to think that these were probably here two thousand years before the Greek colonnades."

Myra changed the topic abruptly as something made her curious, "But why do these marble pieces have a large hole in them?"

"The general theory is that, as the region is earthquake-prone, they used wooden members to keep things from moving and falling on someone. These wooden members would have been slid into these holes," Reeya explained. "Civilisation's first example of earthquake proofing."

They continued past the colonnade and up a flight of stairs, reaching a large plateau. It was dawn, and the orange glow over the horizon was just enough to provide a beautiful sun-kissed view of the surroundings. The stubs of the ruins were now more visible. The greater complexity of ruins and the elevated plateau indicated that this had been an important and central location in the ancient city.

Slowly but surely, the layout was starting to look familiar from the recollection of her previous tour, and she was now feeling more confident in leading the way. The remaining party followed in her footsteps. Kabir kept scanning the distant horizons along with those who accompanied him. They soon reached the stub of a wall that must have been a unique structure in its time. It was the only round structure, connected to an oval one.

"This round structure was most likely the bedroom of someone important. The oval chamber attached may have been a room for meetings with the council or people in general," Reeya restarted her commentary, this time about their standardised weights and linear measures system[154] and how the extensive commerce with surrounding civilisations made them a central hub of sorts.

She looked at the round structure once more and reflected, "To think that someone who slept in that bedroom may have actually had more sway on how human civilisation evolved than most known personalities who came after them," she said. The thought sent a shiver down her spine.

They continued their trek through the ruins, marvelling at the intricately planned settlement for a large population. They turned to the right and headed to an opening in the remains of the stone wall leading to what must have been a grand stadium at the time. Reeya guided the team down the steps that took them closer to the large open space.

"This is the north gate," Reeya announced as she continued down the steps. It opened to an area that seemed like a box in a stadium.

"This is the area from where, it is believed, the more accomplished members of the society would watch whatever games were played in the arena below," she said, indicating the large space ahead of them.

Figure 8: *The "Ten Indus Scripts" discovered near the northern gateway of the Dholavira citadel*

She then pointed to the left, where a tall scoreboard seemed to have been located. "There was a large, 3' x 5' signboard[155] recovered from here. A signboard overlooking the arena and the bleachers on the opposite end could suggest that the common people could read.

"And based on their ability to do complex town planning and engage in trade and commerce, it would be safe to say, a significant portion of the population was literate."

"What did the sign say?" Kabir asked curiously.

"We don't know, the script not having been deciphered. 'No Littering. Keep our metropolis clean', maybe," Reeya said with a smile. "But it is now believed that it was indeed a script, as the same set of symbols is repeated in multiple locations. Also, since they get squished to the right, we can infer that it was written left to right. I hope more resources are poured into deciphering it. It would be quite a day when we learn about the largest and the most complex of ancient civilisations in greater detail."

They passed through an open space that must have served as an amphitheatre or a stadium. Possibly the oldest one known to mankind[156]. She continued through an area criss-crossed with remains of uniformly sized houses along straight streets of equal width. "This part is the middle town. We need to continue through it towards the Manhar river," Reeya said.

"Myra, I suggest you ask your sniper to take position on higher ground. We will be in a vulnerable position when we are near the river," Kabir suggested as he looked around to see the possible approaches Ezio could take.

Myra nodded to one of her men, who acknowledged with a nod. Without a word being exchanged, he took off the heavy sack that resembled a golf bag and placed it on the ground. Kabir picked it up and placed it on his shoulders. The man then headed to higher ground, carrying his rifle and some ammunition.

Reeya broke into a jog as they neared the location and paused at the last piece of wall near the river. She read the distances indicated on the tablet. "They have used the *Baudhyana* theorem to establish a right-angle triangle from this corner of the wall[157]," Reeya inferred, but did not feel the need to explain that it was the older version of the Pythagoras theorem, as she focused on converting the measure to modern units. Studying the ruins, she quickly triangulated the location indicated, using the measuring tape that Myra had come prepared with.

She was thankful that whoever had hidden the steel vessel had indicated the location in relation to the ruins and not the river. Water bodies tend to erode the banks over time, and would have made a very unreliable reference point.

The sun was now higher in the sky, and even though it wasn't warm, the humidity in the air was making everyone feel drained. Reeya made some more calculations and marked a spot on the ground with her feet. "Here. This is where we dig."

The mercenaries saw that as their cue and set down their heavy bags. Opening them, they started to take out the geotechnical drills. Kabir put down the backpack as he watched the two expertly assemble the digging machine.

"You two need to hide. Not much you can do here." Myra was calm as she spoke, "Ezio will be here any minute."

Kabir could sense the coldness in her voice as she anticipated her moment of revenge.

"And take this," Myra said, handing his gun back to Kabir.

He locked eyes with her for a moment as he saw the trust in them. But then, Myra had a sniper somewhere on high ground, in case he pulled any tricks.

They could hear the rumble of a powerful boat approaching the island. He turned to Reeya, who had been scouting for a place to hide. She pointed towards the middle of town as she started running in that direction. He sprinted behind her towards a section of the wall that had tall grass and dense foliage.

Kabir did not like the idea of missing out on the action, but he knew he couldn't be seen near Myra when Ezio arrived. He also felt responsible for Reeya's safety.

Kabir followed Reeya along the wall as they heard the rumble subside. Ezio seemed to have reached the shores of Dholavira.

The metal detector did not show any trace of buried metal, and it made Myra wonder if it was the right spot. But she knew that the vessel was buried quite deep. She'd just have to trust Reeya's judgement and ability to accurately triangulate.

The geotechnical drill was assembled over the little mark that Reeya had made. The men had secured the machine and pulled the lever to activate it. The soft thumping of the digging machine could be heard at a distance as the heavy forged steel drill bit made its way deep into the ground.

Myra had not expected to see Ezio come in with a small army. Maybe a few bodyguards, but not a mini platoon. She felt doomed. She would have to come up with a plan if she wanted to kill Ezio.

Ezio and his men came in and quickly and mechanically spread across the area to secure the perimeter. Ezio was so close to having reached his goal. Despite the dark shades, Myra could see the triumph in his eyes. Ezio's large body and imposing demeanour always made Myra uneasy. It took an effort for her to keep her composure.

"You did ask me to come here quickly because you couldn't handle the heat," Ezio replied tauntingly. "Where is the trouble?" He was expecting a small gunfight at the least.

"We managed to incapacitate them, at least for a while. I see you have brought an army. Expecting that much trouble?" Myra said over the noise of the digging machine.

Ezio ignored the question. "How much longer? The intelligence unit will be here in about two hours. If I don't have the artefact in my hand by then, I'll be taking your head with me instead."

It was not the first time Myra had heard those words. The thought of how casually Ezio made such threats made her stomach churn. She had to grit her teeth not to let her feelings overpower her when she thought he had actually executed them on her boyfriend.

"If you're so afraid of a few men coming for you, feel free to get your men a shovel and help speed up the digging." She feigned a smile and mocked him sarcastically, "Go make yourself useful and find out how far the intelligence unit is."

Ezio was used to such exchanges with Myra and gloatingly let her know that he was in control of the situation. "They should be landing at the Kutch airport right about now. It gives us a little over an hour."

But it was soon evident that Ezio was misinformed. A bullet hitting one of his men made that clear. His anger at his miscalculation manifested in his barking the question at Myra as he ducked for cover, "How deep is the hole now?"

Myra was also taken by surprise as she had not expected the intelligence unit so quickly either. She hoped they were not aiming for her, but ducked to stay clear of stray bullets.

"We are about 2.5 metres down. Nearly halfway. You need to stall them for about an hour," she said to Ezio over the noise of the gunfire.

Ezio's army rallied and concentrated their firepower in the direction from which they were being attacked. The artillery was fully engaged. From machine guns to high-powered rifles, every weapon was trained in the direction of the intelligence unit and fired continuously.

Ezio commanded his men to form a defensive barrier and make sure no one came through. He instructed some of his men to take forward positions to slow down the enemy's march.

"Kill each one of them!" he yelled. "I don't want the perimeter breached."

Then he quickly fell to the ground and crawled to a group of men holding a thick nylon container with a zipper that ran all the way to the bottom. "Arm it now! And reshape the explosive for damage in all directions."

Two men got to work immediately. They opened the container to reveal a metal object made of a series of cylinders. While one started removing the cylinders carefully, the other one punched a code on a small panel at the top.

Myra could see it was intended to be a unidirectional bomb, for shortening the digging time. The explosive compartments were visible when the cylinders were removed. Ezio meant to use it in the hole being dug, and there was nothing she could do to stop him without raising his suspicions.

Nair and his men held their position and continued the attack from the west of where Ezio and his men stood. He signalled to his men to encircle the area from the north, using the stub wall as a shield from the hail of bullets.

Kabir and Reeya had found an outcrop of the wall that served quite well as a shield from any stray bullets. The acacia tree and bushes provided a visual cover without hindering their line of vision.

Kabir whispered to Reeya, "You see, in real life, the reinforcements actually show up in time and not when it is all over." He was obviously proud to be part of the professional and well-oiled organisation. Reeya felt relieved as well.

Suddenly, through the bushes, Kabir saw two people working on a long, cylindrical object. From experience, he knew it was a bomb, with an explosive charge shaped to dig tunnels into rocks. He had to stop it, even if it meant he had to come out of hiding. He had to risk it, as once the bomb was dropped in the hole being dug, it would not be possible to reach it. There was no telling what kind of destruction it might cause. He needed to distract Ezio's men.

Kabir called Nair on his coms device. "What took you so long?" Kabir said jokingly but didn't wait for a reply, "They are assembling an explosive device right behind the outcrop, near the digging machine. Can you hit them with a rocket launcher?"

"Let me see what we can do," Nair assured Kabir and then turned to his team to provide more instructions.

"Hurry up and set up the rocket launcher. We need to hit that outcrop right there." He pointed in the direction that Kabir had described. With a flurry of activity, a rocket launcher was assembled and loaded.

Meanwhile, Ezio was shouting orders to his troops as he orchestrated a defensive position. He pointed to two of his men to provide cover so the digging machine could be removed, and the hole primed to receive the explosive.

The two men immediately signalled to two others to shower bullets to provide them with cover so they could take bullet-proof shields toward the digger. Pulling on the lever, they disengaged the drill from the harness that attached it to the stand. They let the drill bit fall into the hole and removed the attached chuck from the hole, leaving it clear. Ezio was yelling at the detonation expert to hurry up and drop the explosives into the hole.

Kabir put a hand on Reeya, and meeting her gaze, he said with a slight nod. "You stay here. I'm going to stop them from getting that device into the hole."

Reeya nodded. In a smooth motion with his left hand, Kabir removed the gun's safety catch and moved stealthily towards the team about to activate the explosive. He aimed for the guy holding the bomb, and while still moving forward, shot him right through his heart. As he fell, the side of the cylindrical bomb he was carrying slipped onto the ground. The mercenary holding the other end stood frozen in front of Kabir, expecting the next bullet to hit him.

Ezio did not expect anyone to come from that direction, and the sound of the shot startled him. He instantly turned to find that Kabir had shot one of his men. In an almost choreographed move, he picked up his light machine gun and started spraying bullets towards Kabir as he ducked behind a tree.

The man holding the other side of the bomb, realising a window of opportunity, dragged the cylinder towards the open hole. The dirt and the grass did not offer much resistance, allowing him to get into position quickly. He still had to heave the cylinder to make it stand vertically and activate the detonator switch before he could slip it into the hole.

Kabir realised he had missed the opportunity to take out the second man carrying the bomb. He tried looking for an alternate place to take cover, but could see nothing. It was impossible to move from behind the large tree trunk and run, as he was directly in Ezio's line of fire.

Seconds seemed like an eternity to Kabir as he waited, hoping for the blast from the rocket launcher. In his mind, he plotted each player on the battlefield, searching for events that would lead to an opportune moment.

What followed was almost simultaneous. The grenade from the launcher exploded just behind the mercenary holding the cylinder. The explosion thrust him forward as the shockwave lifted his body in the air and pushed him against the cylinder he was heaving. It was the last push that was needed. The cylinder slipped from his hands and fell vertically into the hole, as his limp body fell to the ground.

Ezio could see the cylinder slip into place. The rocket from the launcher had thrown him against Myra. Even though the explosion was far from him, he could feel the scorching heat burn his skin. In that moment of searing pain, he also felt the anguish of seeing the bomb fall into the hole dug in the ground. He had wanted the artefact for himself. He had known that he would control the world's energy market if he could learn from what had been made over two thousand years ago. He understood that he must destroy his cauldron and not let it fall into his enemy's hands. It still pained him as he saw his dream slip away, and he realised that the explosion from the cylinder would destroy whatever was buried deep in the hole. The satisfaction that no one else would have it somehow wasn't enough.

Myra had been shielded from the explosion with Ezio standing between her and the blast. The sound, heat and dust cloud made everything hazy. Myra knew this was her opportunity. She let her instincts take over. Taking out her hunting knife from its leather sheath, she exposed the titanium-coated razor-sharp blade with a flick of her thumb.

Her body was already in motion to counter Ezio's weight, which would topple into her. In a split second, her hand reached his throat. Expertly, she thrust the sharp blade into Ezio's jugular and pulled it out as his body fell backwards, jumping out of the way as blood gushed out of Ezio's throat.

His eyes were still open as he hit the ground and stared at Myra, as if asking 'why?' Myra wanted to tell him before he closed his eyes forever. She knew she only had a few seconds. She also knew that the cylinder that had gone into the hole would explode any second. It was a risk she was willing to take.

Looking into Ezio's eyes, she said, "Novak was my boyfriend and a loyal soldier to you. It was your own wife who used his phone to frame him." Myra knew he could hear her. The severed artery would have stopped carrying blood to his brain, but even as his world darkened, hers would be the final words he would hear. She did not have the luxury to savour the moment, but the peace of mind she had thought she would get by avenging Novak's death still eluded her.

She knew one of Ezio's men would have seen her kill him. She moved quickly, turning away from Ezio's body while keeping her head low to avoid bullets. She sprinted towards the stub of a wall and dived behind it to get cover.

Kabir had emerged from behind the tree just in time to see Myra sprinting away from Ezio's body. The blood oozing from Ezio's neck was enough to tell Kabir what had happened. He spotted Ezio's bodyguard aiming his gun at Myra as she ran. Kabir took aim and squeezed the trigger multiple times. The bodyguard convulsed and fell to the ground.

"Run! Take cover!" Myra turned around and yelled at Kabir. Kabir ran towards the bomb, hoping there was a way to defuse it. To stop it. Or minimise damage.

"You have five seconds!" Myra yelled as she ran towards a large rock.

"Hurry! You cannot stop it!" Reeya heard Myra and yelled as she came out from behind her cover.

Seeing Reeya exposed, Kabir ran towards her through the bullets that were still flying between the two sides. He had to reach her and get her behind that wall in the few seconds remaining before the explosion. While still running, he grabbed Reeya and dived behind the rock wall. The only thought in his mind was that he couldn't lose Reeya to the explosion. He landed on his side as he shielded Reeya from the impact.

The explosion was powerful and loud. Dirt erupted from the hole and travelled several meters up in the air. The earth rumbled and rolled beneath Kabir. Ezio's men, who had been standing near the hole, were swallowed up by the newly formed crater.

Nair and his men watched the enormous cloud billowing skywards. They all stood rooted to the ground before debris came raining down, scattering everyone. The sporadic shooting continued, but Nair and his men picked out the rest of Ezio's army, one by one.

"Reeya, talk to me. Are you okay?" Reeya stood stupefied. Kabir held her in his arms and then shook her gently by the shoulders.

"It's gone. Did it get destroyed?" Reeya said sadly. She wasn't sure if the explosion had been deep enough, but she sounded resigned as she examined the crater.

Nair reached the crater with some of his men and looked down as the rest of the team gathered up Ezio's remaining men.

"Where is Myra?" asked Kabir, looking around. He was quite sure she had escaped the blast and run in the direction he thought she had gone.

As he climbed down a hill to reach the shore of the island, he saw the salt-laden, thick wake of a boat, with the vessel itself barely visible on the horizon. He knew that Myra had escaped. But she had delivered on her promise to him. Much as it pained Kabir, he chose to walk back at a leisurely pace to inform Nair that Myra had escaped, giving her enough time to disappear.

19

Rakhigarhi

THE DAY HAD BEEN A BLUR FOR KABIR AND REEYA.

Soon after the explosion, all of Ezio's men had either been killed or had surrendered. Myra had managed to get into Ezio's boat along with some of her soldiers, and Kabir had only seen the wake of the boat as she vanished into the horizon. Nair had tried to debrief the chief on the events of Khadir island, but was surprised when he was asked to secure the site and leave it to the task force that was coming.

"There is a joint task force that has been dispatched. These are members of the Department of Atomic Energy (DAE) and the Bhabha Atomic Research Centre (BARC). They will be taking over from you," Singh had informed Nair tersely.

Nair had tried to protest, "There is a crater and dead bodies all over. How can we leave all the carnage to the DAE and BARC folks?"

"They are capable agencies and know what they are doing. These orders have come directly from the Home Ministry. It's out of my hands now."

"You do realise that if this artefact is found, it is going to be a big deal. Not only would it prove that a thorium MSR reaction was done in the past, but it might also give us some concrete information on what materials to use," Nair protested.

"And even if it does not, it will educate the people who protest without knowing the complete picture. We need to inform people that certain types of fission are inherently safe and don't necessarily translate to a nuclear meltdown. That with the right investments, it can prove to be a green and economical alternative. Even Ezio had big plans to profit from the find," Nair continued, trying to convince Singh, but to no avail.

Reeya and Kabir, along with the rest of the team, flew back to Delhi, where the large, black SUVs were already waiting for them when they landed. Kabir and Reeya did not see the need to go with Nair, but he insisted as he ushered them into the SUV with him. They still had a mole to find!

As the SUV rolled into the underground garage of the intelligence headquarters, Singh's team was waiting to go and arrest the mole. Ritvik was just sitting at his desk, expressionless. He knew his cover was blown. Singh was rather surprised at the calm he displayed; he had thought Ritvik would be trying to escape.

"Why did I do it?" Ritvik said, still stone-faced. "I don't think you'd understand."

"Not that it matters, but try me," the chief tried to be empathetic. He was curious to know what could motivate a person like Ritvik to work with someone like Ezio.

Ritvik looked at Singh, wondering if he should explain himself or just leave it a mystery. As the deputy chief, Kabir and Reeya walked in, he pursed his lips to indicate he wanted to have the discussion in private.

"Wait for me in the conference room. I'm expecting a call and will be there shortly," Singh told the trio, as he turned back to face Ritvik.

"Do you know how long it has been since we have known that we, as a country, can lead the thorium MSR technology and enable a green and energy-independent world?" Ritvik said after a long, deliberate pause.

"All of us at the agency work long hours with meagre salaries, to keep our country safe. To work towards us being a force to be reckoned with. But is that enough?" It was obvious Ritvik was passionate about his cause. "Can we not expect the decision-makers of this country to do their job and move us to leadership positions in areas where we may prove to be more advantageous?" Ritvik demanded.

"I know that we as a country are unlikely to do much with this technology. The bureaucrats will take too long to analyse. The politicians will take too long to decide. The ministries will take too long to release funds. By then, someone will swoop in and replicate what is rightfully ours!" Ritvik seemed like a bitter man who had given it good thought.

"I knew that Ezio had the capital and the lust to develop this technology. He would have taken the artefact and dissected it till he had the know-how to make it work. Yes, he'd have done it for greed, but it would have happened... And no. I did not do it for the money."

Singh wished that he could argue convincingly against what Ritvik was saying, but he knew there was no winning this argument.

"I only wish we could prove you wrong. I get the feeling that DAE and BARC will show us a miracle in a few years that none of us expect," Singh said, trying his best to add conviction to his voice.

It was not going to be an easy task. He hoped to find out more about the artefact in his next meeting. Silently, he left Ritvik sitting and proceeded to join the trio. Nair, Reeya and Kabir were already in the conference room waiting for the chief.

"Your idea of splitting the information to identify the mole was ingenious," Singh complimented Nair. "Only Ritvik could have deduced your destination was Kutch. Ezio had enough time before you would show up with your team."

"It pains me to think that our own people feel that outsiders can out-invest us and take a leadership role in a green energy technology," he said, softly shaking his head.

The large wall monitor came to life, and Momita came on, looking excited.

"Have your people been able to locate the artefact? Did it survive the explosion?" Reeya asked. Having been briefed about the DEA spokesperson, could not contain her curiosity.

"I would not be able to comment on that," said Momita evasively. "But I do want to thank you and Kabir for all your hard work and the risks you took. I am also thankful that we were brought in early enough so we could be well prepared."

"Well prepared for what?" asked Kabir, trying to get some answers.

"I cannot tell you that," Momita said with a smile, seemingly enjoying keeping everyone in suspense. After a thoughtful pause, she said, "We are aware that we need to step up and take a leadership role in solving the energy needs of the world. We are already working on thorium MSR with scientists from all over the world. The rumour that such a technology existed in the past will inspire us all to accelerate the process. We have also learned that Ezio and others like him can help and may lead us to a more collaborative way of working with the public in general."

Kabir knew that was about as much as he was going to learn from Momita. He could also feel the exhaustion set in and thought it was time to head home.

"Do you think they know what happened to Myra?" Reeya asked curiously.

"I'm sure they do. I'm also sure that we've not seen the last of her," Kabir said.

Reeya was wary of the turboprop that was waiting to take them back to Rajgir. Nair came out of the car carrying a tiffin to thank Reeya and Kabir.

"This food is just about the only good thing on the plane. But I'm glad to be headed back," Reeya said with a smile.

Nair smiled. "There is more where that came from. You should come home sometime."

"And that reminds me, I should leave these with you," Reeya said, handing over the wootz piece and the cut retort to the deputy chief as she started to move towards the plane.

"Oh, and there is a new dig happening in Rakhigarhi that may be of interest," Nair said as his voice got lost under the noise of the engine. But he knew they had both heard as he caught them exchanging glances with a smile.

The duo strapped themselves in as the plane took off. As they settled into their seats, it dawned on Kabir that the adventure was over. More than the action, he knew he was going to miss Reeya.

Just as he was trying to think up excuses to meet her again, Reeya put her head against Kabir's shoulder and casually took his hand.

"What do you think Mr Nair meant by the new excavation?"

Table of Figures

End Notes

1 John Marshall, "Rajagrha and Its Remains," ASI-AR, 1905-06 (Delhi: Swati Publications, 1990), 102. "The lowest stratum revealed two clay seals, bearing short illegible epigraphs in characters of the first or second century B.C."

2 Sudha Satyawadi, *Proto-Historic Pottery of Indus Valley Civilization—Study of Painted Motifs* (New Delhi: D. K. Print World Pvt. Ltd., 1994), col. illus. 16: "Kalibanga, fish scale pattern on it from Kalibanga, ASI collection, Purana Qila."

3 *Fragment of a Chainmail Armor*, Metal Alloy, 9th-10th century CE, Acc. No. NM 08081, Nalanda Museum, Bihar.

4 B. N. Mishra, *Nalanda: Sources and Background*, vol. 1 (Delhi: B. R. Publishing Corporation, 1998), 181-182.

5 *Text from Nidana or Pratittya Samutpada Sutra in Brahmi Script*, Terracotta, 6th century CE, Nalanda Museum, Bihar.

6 B. R. Mani, "Rajagriha," *History of Ancient India*, vol. VII, ed. Dilip K. Chakrabarti and Makkhan Lal (Delhi: Vivekanand International Foundation and Aryan Books, 2014), 602.

7 Frederick M. Asher, *Nalanda: Situating the Great Monastery* (Mumbai: The Marg Foundation, 2015), 104-05.

8 John Marshall, "Rajagrha and Its Remains," *ASI-AR* 1905-06 (Delhi: Swati Publications, 1990), 88.

9 Shrikant Singh, "Rajgriha in Historical Perspective with Special Reference to Chinese Pilgrims," *India's Perception through Chinese Travellers*, ed. Ravindra Panth (Bihar: Nava Nalanda Mahavihar, 2007), 65.

10 V. H. Jackson, "Notes on Old Rajagriha," *ASI-AR* 1913-14, ed. John Marshall et al. (Delhi: Swati Publications, 1990), 265.

11 B. R. Mani, "Rajagriha," *History of Ancient India,* vol. II (Delhi: Vivekanand International Foundation and Aryan Books, 2014), 606.

12 B. C. Law, "Rajagriha in Ancient Literature," *Memoirs of ASI,* No. 58 (Reprint, Delhi: Swati Publications, 1991), 41.

13 Brajmohan Kumar, *Archaeology of Patliputra and Nalanda* (Delhi: Ramanand Vidya Bhawan, 1987), 14.

14 J. L. Mehta and Sarita Mehta, *History of Ancient India* (New Delhi: Lotus Press, 2008), 226.

15 B. N. Mishra, *Nalanda: Sources and Background*, vol. 1 (Delhi: B. R. Publishing Corporation, 1998), 181.

16 Mishra, *Nalanda: Sources and Background,* 181.

17 Mishra, *Nalanda: Sources and Background*, 182.

18 H. D. Sankalia, *The Nalanda University* (Delhi: Oriental Publishers, 1972), 195: Hieun Tsang's biographer, Shaman Hwui Li, however, sheds more light on a number of students in Nalanda. He writes, "The Sangharamas of India are counted by myriads, but this is the most remarkable for grandeur and height. The priests, belonging to the convent,

or strangers (residing therein), always reach the number of 10,000." That all these occupants were students is clear from the lines that follow.

19 H. D. Sankalia, *The Nalanda University* (Delhi: Oriental Publishers, 1972), 220.

20 John Marshall, *Taxila: An Illustrated Account of Archaeological Excavations*, vol. I (Delhi: Bhartiya Publishing House, 1975), 11.

21 H. D. Sankalia, *The Nalanda University* (Delhi: Oriental Publishers, 1972), 249.

22 Sankalia, *The Nalanda University*, 7-9.

23 B. N. Mishra, *Nalanda: Sources and Background*, vol. 1 (Delhi: B. R. Publishing Corporation, 1998), 191.

24 Mishra, *Nalanda: Sources and Background*, 193-194: "A partial destruction of Nalanda was caused by several wars during the period of later Guptas and Varmanas. Jayanaga of the Naga dynasty ruling in Gauda. He appointed Sasanka as the governor of Magadha. Sasanka razed the buildings of Nalanda and murdered its inhabitants or dispersed them."

25 H. D. Sankalia, *The Nalanda University* (Delhi: Oriental Publishers, 1972), 61: "Harsa built a great *sangharama* at Nalanda. But he also constructed a *vihara* with brass plates and a high wall round all the buildings."

26 J.K. Sharma, "The Perception of Nalanda Through Chinese Travellers," *India's Perception through Chinese Travellers*, ed. Ravindra Panth (Bihar: Nava Nalanda Mahavihar, 2007), 7.

27 Yogendra Singh, "Chinese Travellers and their Purpose of Journey," *India's Perception through Chinese Travellers*, ed. Ravindra Panth (Bihar: Nava Nalanda Mahavihar, 2007), 47.

28 H. D. Sankalia, *The Nalanda University* (Delhi: Oriental Publishers, 1972), 245.

29 Brajmohan Kumar, *Archaeology of Patliputra and Nalanda* (Delhi: Ramanand Vidya Bhawan, 1987), 37: "According to Minhaj, the author of *Tabaqat-i-Nasiri*, there were only 200 horsemen defending the Mahavihar. The slaughter of the shaven-headed Brahmanas, as the Muslim chronicler calls the Buddhist monk, was so complete that when the victor searched for someone capable of explaining the contents of the libraries, not a single living monk could be found. On being acquainted with the contents of these books, it was found that the whole of that fortress and city was a place of learning. A similar fate befell the other Buddhist institutions at Nalanda, which became targets of the combined intolerance and rapacity of the invaders."

30 H. D. Sankalia, *The Nalanda University* (Delhi: Oriental Publishers, 1972), 246: "The tradition cited from *Pag-sam-jonzang* about the final annihilation of Nalanda by fire may be true, for, while excavating the Nalanda site, heaps of ashes and coals are unearthed, even on the topmost levels after the removal of layers of earth which cover up various sites."

31 J.K. Sharma, "The Perception of Nalanda Through Chinese Travellers," *India's Perception through Chinese Travellers*, ed. Ravindra Panth (Bihar: Nava Nalanda Mahavihar, 2007), 5. "The Indian visits of Hieun-tsang (629-645 AD) and I-tsing (671-695 AD) are of great significance because they have left behind some really useful account of the Buddhist monastic education in India in general and Nalanda in particular, which has been excavated from the mound of village Baragaon, about some 100 km from Patna, and 10 km from Rajgir."

32 H. D. Sankalia, *The Nalanda University* (Delhi: Oriental Publishers, 1972), 72-73. "According to Tibetan accounts, moreover, Nalanda had a grand library, called Dharmaganja (Piety Mart). It consisted of three grand buildings called Ratnasagara, Ratnodadhi and Ratnaranjaka, respectively. In Ratnodadhi, which was nine-storeyed, there were the sacred scripts called *Prajnaparamita-sutra* and Tantric works."

33 B. N. Mishra, *Nalanda: Art*, vol. 2 (Delhi: B. R. Publishing Corporation, 1998), 191.

34 J. S. Park, et al. "High Carbon Steel and Ancient Sword Making as Observed in a Double Edged Sword from an Iron Age Megalithic Burial in Tamil Nadu, India," *Archeometry 62- 1* (2020), 77-78.

35 T. R. Anantharaman, *The Rustless Wonder: A Study of the Iron Pillar at Delhi* (Delhi: Vigyan Prasar Publication, 1996), 6. "There is, however, very strong and reliable evidence that after the second century A.D., trading was carried out in Indian steel, and this became a well-recognised commodity for the making of swords and armour in Persia, the Middle East and Arab countries."

36 S. Srinivasan and S. Ranganathan, *India's Legendary Wootz Steel: An Advanced Material of the Ancient World* (Hyderabad: University Press India Private Limited, 2014), 50.

37 K.T.M. Hegde, *An Introduction to Ancient Indian Metallurgy* (Bangalore: Geological Society of India, 1991), 51-52.

38 S. Srinivasan and S. Ranganathan, *India's Legendary Wootz Steel: An Advanced Material of the Ancient World* (Hyderabad: University Press India Private Limited, 2014), 47.

39 R. Balasubramaniam, *Marvels of Indian Iron through the Ages* (Delhi: Rupa and Co., 2008), 254.

40 K.T.M. Hegde, *An Introduction to Ancient Indian Metallurgy* (Bangalore: Geological Society of India, 1991), 50.

41 R. Balasubramaniam, *Marvels of Indian Iron through the Ages* (Delhi: Rupa and Co., 2008), 232.

42 R. Balasubramaniam, *The World Heritage Complex of the Qutub* (New Delhi: Aryan Books International, 2005), 35.

43 Balasubramaniam, *The World Heritage Complex of the Qutub*, 42.

44 Balasubramaniam, *The World Heritage Complex of the Qutub*, 41: "The original erection site of the Delhi Iron Pillar at Udayagiri has been recently deduced based on epigraphic and archaeological evidence. This location is in front of the passageway, ahead of cave 7."

45 Brajmohan Kumar, *Archaeology of Patliputra and Nalanda* (Delhi: Ramanand Vidya Bhawan, 1987), 17. Udayi, the son and successor of Ajatsatru, who ruled from 430- 364 BCE, transferred his capital from Rajgrha to Patliputra.

46 Kumar, *Archaeology of Patliputra and Nalanda*, 19. Chandragupta established a new dynasty, the Mauryas, with the help and advice of Chanakya in 324 BCE.

47 Percy Brown, *Indian Architecture: Buddhist and Hindu* (Bombay: D.B. Taraporevala Sons, 1956), 5.

48 R. Balasubramanayam, *The World Heritage Complex of the Qutub* (New Delhi: Aryan Books International, 2005), 37.

49 D. R. Patil, "The Monuments of Udaygiri Hill," *Discovering Vidisha: Art, Archaeology and Architecture*, ed. Yogendra Sharma and Om Prakash Mishra (New Delhi: Aryan Books International, 2010), 104.

50 R. Balasubramanayam, *The World Heritage Complex of the Qutub* (New Delhi: Aryan Books International, 2005), 36.

51 D. R. Patil, "The Monuments of Udaygiri Hill," *Discovering Vidisha: Art, Archaeology and Architecture*, ed. Yogendra Sharma and Om Prakash Mishra (New Delhi: Aryan Books International, 2010), 104.

52 K.T.M. Hegde, *An Introduction to Ancient Indian Metallurgy* (Bangalore: Geological Society of India, 1991), 53-54.

53 Vibha Tripathi, *History of Iron Technology in India: From Beginning to Pre-Modern Times* (New Delhi: Rupa & Co., 2008), 72.

54 R. Balasubramanayam, *The World Heritage Complex of the Qutub* (New Delhi: Aryan Books International, 2005), 41.

55 S. K. Tiwari, *Riddles of Indian Rockshelter Paintings* (New Delhi: Sarup & Sons, 2000), 189.

56 Y. S. Rawat, "Coastal Sites: Possible Port Towns of Harappan time in Gujarat," *Port Towns of Gujarat*, ed. Sara Keller and Michael Pearson (New Delhi: Primus Books, 2015), 187.

57 Vasant Shinde et al., "An Ancient Harappan Genome Lacks Ancestry from Steppe Pastoralists or Iranian Farmers," *Cell* (2019). https://doi.org/10.1016/j.cell.2019.08.048

58 B P Sinha, *Readings in Kautilya's Arthashashtra* (Delhi: Agam Prakashan, 1976), 154-158.

59 B C Sinha, *Studies in Alexander's Campaigns* (Varanasi: Bhartiya Publishing House, 1973), 18-19. "After conquering Suso, he marched towards Persepolis. It was the 'richest of all the cities under the Sun'. It was the real capital of the Persian kings. The city was sacked and burnt. Alexander might have done it as a mark of the decisive overthrow of the Persian Empire. But this cruelty cannot be defended."

60 Prakash Chandra Prasad, *Foreign Trade and Commerce in Ancient India* (New Delhi: Abhinav Publication, 1977), 29.

61 Nagendra Nath Ghosh, *Early History of India* (Allahabad: The Indian Press, 1951), 101. "At this point, Alexander met with his first and strongest opposition from an Indian power, King Porus, the Paurava king of the country between the Jhelum and Chenab"

62 B C Sinha, *Studies in Alexander's Campaigns* (Varanasi: Bhartiya Publishing House, 1973), 40-41.

63 S. Srinivasan and S. Ranganathan, *India's Legendary Wootz Steel: An Advanced Material of the Ancient World* (Hyderabad: University Press India Private Limited, 2014), 52.

64 D. R. Patil, "The Monuments of Udaygiri Hill," *Discovering Vidisha: Art, Archaeology and Architecture*, ed. Yogendra Sharma and Om Prakash Mishra (New Delhi: Aryan Books International, 2010), 120.

65 Patil, "The Monuments of Udaygiri Hill," *Discovering Vidisha: Art, Archaeology and Architecture*, 120-21.

66 Patil, "The Monuments of Udaygiri Hill," *Discovering Vidisha: Art, Archaeology and Architecture*, 113.

67 Patil, "The Monuments of Udaygiri Hill," *Discovering Vidisha: Art, Archaeology and Architecture*, 107.

68 Patil, "The Monuments of Udaygiri Hill," *Discovering Vidisha: Art, Archaeology and Architecture*, 120. "The inscription in the Cave No. 6 of the Gupta era 82 (402 CE) is the earliest dated inscription of the Gupta period."

69 D. R. Patil, "The Monuments of Udaygiri Hill," *Discovering Vidisha: Art, Archaeology and Architecture*, ed. Yogendra Sharma and Om Prakash Mishra (New Delhi: Aryan Books International, 2010), 110.

70 P. T. Craddock et. al., "Ancient Industry of Lead, Silver & Zinc in Rajasthan," *Archaeometallurgy in India*, ed. Vibha Tripathi (Delhi: Sharada Publishing House, 1998), 125.

71 Percy Brown, *Indian Architecture: Buddhist and Hindu* (Bombay: D.B. Taraporevala Sons, 1956), 18.

72 Brown, *Indian Architecture: Buddhist and Hindu*, 15.

73 Ananda K. Coomaraswamy, *Yaksas: Part 1* (New Delhi: Munshiram Manoharlal: 1971), 7. "...they possess the power of assuming any shape, the female particularly that of a very beautiful woman (so that an unknown beauty is asked if she be the goddess of the district, or a Yaksi); they are kindly, but can fight fiercely as guardians..."

74 Coomaraswamy, *Yaksas: Part 1*, 9.

75 F. C. Maisey, *Sanchi and its Remains*, (Varanasi: Indological Book House, 1972), 53.

76 Maisey, *Sanchi and its Remains*, 51-52.

77 Maisey, *Sanchi and its Remains*, 49-50.

78 Maisey, *Sanchi and its Remains*, 53.

79 Percy Brown, *Indian Architecture: Buddhist and Hindu*, (Bombay: D.B. Taraporevala Sons, 1956), 15.

80 A. Cunningham, *The Bhilsa Topes: Buddhist Monuments of Central India*, ed. B. M. Pande (New Delhi: Aryan Books International, 2009), 115.

81 Percy Brown, *Indian Architecture: Buddhist and Hindu* (Bombay: D.B. Taraporevala Sons, 1956), 5. Conjectural reconstruction of the main gateway of the ancient city of Kushinagar (c. 500 BCE) in Magadha, Bihar. Adapted from a bas-relief on the Southern Gateway of the Great Stupa of Sanchi.

82 F. C. Maisey, *Sanchi and its Remains* (Varanasi: Indological Book House, 1972), 53.

83 Maisey, *Sanchi and its Remains*, 51.

84 Debala Mitra, *Sanchi* (New Delhi: Archaeological Survey of India, 1965), 50. "Temple 17 is a remarkable piece of Gupta architecture, noted for its structural propriety, symmetry, logical proportions and restraint in ornamentation."

85 T. R. Anantharaman, *The Rustless Wonder: A Study of the Iron Pillar at Delhi* (Delhi: Vigyan Prasar, 1996), 71.

86 Percy Brown, *Indian Architecture: Buddhist and Hindu* (Mumbai: D B Taraporevala Sons: 1956), 17. "The inscription states that it was a *Garuda* pillar raised in honour of the god Vasudeva by Heliodorus, son of Dion, who was a resident of Taxila and had come to the court of the local prince Bhagabhadra as an envoy from the Indo-Bactrian king Antialkidas. In these few lines a whole chapter of early history is condensed pointing to the relations that existed between this part of India and the Greek kingdoms of the Punjab, as well as to the fact that Heliodorus, a Greek, had adopted an Indian faith, and the inclusion of the name Antialkidas gives 140 B.C., as the approximate date of its erection."

87 Suniti Kumar Chatterji, "Brahmi – The Mother of Indian Scripts," *Devnagari Through the Ages* (Delhi: Central Hindi Directorate, Ministry of Education, Govt. of India, 1967), 7-8.

88 Kim Plofker, *Mathematics in India* (New Jersey: Princeton University Press, 2009), 55.

89 Plofker, *Mathematics in India*, 13-14.

90 Plofker, *Mathematics in India,* 54.

91 Plofker, *Mathematics in India*, 56.

92 B. Lakshmi, "Acharaya Pingalas Maathra Meru," *Prayoga Institute of Education Research,* https://www.prayoga.org.in/post/acharya-pingala-s-maathra-meru.

93 Kim Plofker, *Mathematics in India* (New Jersey: Princeton University Press, 2009), 57.

94 J.S. Kharakwal, *Indian Zinc Technology in a Global Perspective* (Chennai: Infinity Foundation India, 2020), 376. "…*yasada* or *Jasada* of the early Indian texts in Sanskrit have been variously interpreted either as zinc ore or zinc."

95 P. T. Craddock et al., "Ancient Industry of Lead, Silver & Zinc in Rajasthan," *Archaeometallurgy in India*, ed. Vibha Tripathi (Delhi: Sharada Publishing House, 1998), 122.

96 Paul. T. Craddock, *Early Metal Mining and Production* (Washington: Smithsonian Institution Press, 1995), 312.

97 J.S. Kharakwal, L. K. Gurjar, "Zinc and Brass in Archaeological Perspective," *Ancient Asia,* vol. 1 (2006), 144.

98 J.S. Kharakwal, *Indian Zinc Technology in a Global Perspective* (Chennai: Infinity Foundation India, 2020), 439-440.

99 B. C. Mohanty et al., *Natural Dying Processes of India* (Ahmedabad: Calico Museum of Textile, 1987), 149.

100 J. S. Kharakwal and L. K. Gurjar, "Zinc and Brass in Archaeological Perspective," *Ancient Asia*, vol.1 (2006), 154.

101 Kharakwal and Gurjar, "Zinc and Brass in Archaeological Perspective," *Ancient Asia*, vol. 1, 155.

102 Edward D'Cruz, *A Survey of World Civilization* (Bombay: Lalvani Publishing House,1970), 119-120. "Julius Caesar (r.64-44 BCE) saw that Rome and the Roman Empire could be saved only by the strong hand of a single ruler." He is credited with establishing the Roman Empire.

103 B C Sinha, *Studies in Alexander's Campaigns* (Varanasi: Bhartiya Publishing House, 1973), 67.

104 K. T. M. Hegde, *An Introduction to Ancient Indian Metallurgy* (Bangalore: Geological Society of India, 2018), 63. "It is

possible to summarise that the zinc metal-working at Zawar started at least a few centuries earlier than the first century BC."

105 Hegde, *An Introduction to Ancient Indian Metallurgy*, 62.

106 Hegde, *An Introduction to Ancient Indian Metallurgy*, 57.

107 Angus Maddison, *Contours of the World Economy, 1-2030 AD: Essays in Macro-Economic History* (Oxford University Press, 2007), 379.

108 Jim Dobson, "A One Trillion Dollar Hidden Treasure Chamber is Discovered at India's Sree Padmanabhaswamy Temple," *Forbes*, November 13, 2015

https://www.forbes.com/sites/jimdobson/2015/11/13/a-one-trillion-dollar-hidden-treasure-chamber-is-discovered-at-indias-sree-padmanabhaswam-temple/?sh=616eec971ba6.

109 "Once an Indian Ruler was World's Richest Person," *The Business Standard*, January 3, 2021. https://www.tbsnews.net/feature/once-indian-ruler-was-worlds-richest-person-180340

110 B. C. Sinha, "Appendix," *Studies in Alexander's Campaigns* (Varanasi: Bhartiya Publishing House, 1973), 69. From early in May 327 B.C. to September-October 326 B.C.

111 Rupali Patil et al., "Rubia Cordifolia: A Review," *Oriental Pharmacy and Experimental Medicine* 9 (2009), 2. doi:10.3742/OPEM.2009.9.1.001.

112 Jian Liu et al., "Profiling by HPLC-DAD-MSD Reveals a 2500-Year History of the Use of Natural Dyes in Northwest China," *Dyes and Pigments* 187 (March 1, 2021). https://doi.org/10.1016/j.dyepig.2021.109143. "The earliest madder-type dye (most likely Rubia cordifolia) seems to be found in cotton from Mohenjo-Daro in the Indus Valley about 5000 years ago."

113 Shabnam Bano & Wajeeha Begum, "Majeeth (*Rubia codifolia Linn*): A review," *IJARIIT,* vol. 8, Issue 1 (2022), 227. https://www.ijariit.com/manuscripts/v8i1/V8I1-1261.pdf.

114 Richard Saloman, "Writing System of the Indo-Aryan Languages," *The Indo-Aryan Languages*, ed. George Cardona and Dhanesh Jain (London: Routledge Taylor and Francis Group, 2003), 75.

115 V. S. Agrawala, "The Devanagari Script," *Devanagari Through the Ages*, Issue 8 (Delhi: Albion Press, 1967), 14.

116 K.N. Dikshit, "The Decline of Harappan Civilization," *Ancient India,* New Series, No. 1 (New Delhi: Archaeological Survey of India, 2011), 132-133.

117 Alok Kumar Kanungo, et al., "Understanding Ancient Zinc Technologies: An Experimental Study," *Man & Environment XLV-2* (2020), 88. https://asc.iitgn.ac.in/assets/publications/research_papers/Zinc_Extraction_2020.pdf

118 P. T. Craddock et al., "Ancient Industry of Lead, Silver and Zinc in Rajasthan," *Archaeometallurgy in India*, ed. Vibha Tripathi (Delhi: Sharada Publishing House, 1998), 124.

119 J. S. Kharakwal, *Indian Zinc Technology in a Global Perspective* (Chennai: Infinity Foundation, 2020), 437.

120 K. T. M. Hegde, *An Introduction to Ancient Indian Metallurgy* (Bangalore: Geological Society of India, 1991), 63.

121 J. S. Kharakwal, *Indian Zinc Technology in a Global Perspective* (Chennai: Infinity Foundation, 2020), 296.

122 R. Balasubramaniam, *Marvels of Indian Iron through the Ages* (Delhi: Rupa and Company, 2008), 226.

123 Jonathan Mark Kenoyer, "Ancient Cities of the Indus Valley Civilization," *American Anthropologist* (Karachi: Oxford University Press, 1998), 17. "… they are spread out over

680,000 square kilometres of Northwestern South Asia, an area twice the size of ancient Egypt or Mesopotamia."

124 H. D. Sankalia, *The Prehistory and Protohistory of India and Pakistan* (Puna: Shrisaraswati Mudranalaya, 1974), 404.

125 Y.S. Rawat, "Possible Port Towns of Harappan Time in Gujarat," *Port Towns of Gujarat*, ed. Sara Keller and Michael Pearson (Delhi: Primus Books, 2015), 199.

126 K. N. Dikshit, "The Decline of Harappan Civilization," *Ancient India*, New Series, No. 1 (New Delhi: Archaeological Survey of India, 2011), 133. "It is suspected that the decline of the Harappan civilisation was, at least, partly due to the decline in the long-distance trade activities, around 1800 BC, with Mesopotamia and the Persian Gulf."

127 S. Srinivasan and S. Ranganathan, *India's Legendary Wootz Steel: An Advanced Material of the Ancient World* (Hyderabad: University Press India Private Limited, 2014), 51.

128 R. Balasubramaniam, *Marvels of Indian Iron through the Ages* (Delhi: Rupa and Company, 2008), 228. "In the fourth-fifth century BCE, in the Persian Court, Ktesias was presented with two swords of Indian steel by the Malloi."

129 Srinivasan Kalyanaraman, "Tradition of crucible steel traced back to Sarasvati Sindhu CIvilization & Indus Script Corpora, ca. 2500 BCE – A tribute to late Prof. R. Balasubramania," (2020), 16. https://www.academia.edu/44484820/Tradition_of_crucible_steel_traced_back_t1o_Sarasvati_Sindhu_CIvilization_and_Indus_Script_Corpora_A_tribute_to_late_Prof_R_Balasubramaniam

130 S. R. Rao, "Lothal: A Harappan Port Town", *Memoirs of the Archaeological Survey of India*, No. 78, vol. 1 (New Delhi: Archaeological Survey of India, 1979), 221-226.

131 Rao, S. R. "A 'Persian Gulf' Seal from Lothal," *Antiquity* 37, No. 146 (1963), 96–99. doi:10.1017/S0003598X00037194.

132 Y.S. Rawat, "Coastal Sites: Possible Port Towns of Harappan Time in Gujarat," *Port Towns of Gujarat*, ed. Sara Keller and Michael Pearson (Delhi: Primus Books, 2015), 191-192.

133 Jagat Pati Joshi, *Harappan Architecture and Civil Engineering* (New Delhi: Infinity Foundation and Rupa, 2008), 67-68.

134 R. S. Bisht, "Harappan Hydraulic Engineering", *Science and Metal Technology of Harappans* (New Delhi: Kaveri Books, 2012), 197.

135 Jagat Pati Joshi, *Harappan Architecture and Civil Engineering* (New Delhi: Infinity Foundation and Rupa, 2008), 118-119.

136 R. S. Bisht, "Harappan Hydraulic Engineering," *Science and Metal Technology of Harappans* (New Delhi: Kaveri Books, 2012), 195.

137 Chroneos, "Thorium Fuel Revisited," *Progress in Nuclear Energy*, 1.

138 R. B. Hargraves and R. W. Moir, "Liquid Fluoride Thorium Reactors," *American Scientist* 98, No. 4 (2010), 306. https://doi.org/10.1511/2010.85.304.

139 Alexander Chroneos et al., "Thorium Fuel Revisited," *Progress in Nuclear Energy* 164 (October 1, 2023, 3. https://doi.org/10.1016/j.pnucene.2023.104839. "Presently, the UK, China, India and the USA investigate the use of Th for civil nuclear-energy applications."

140 R. B. Hargraves and R.W. Moir, "Liquid Fluoride Thorium Reactors," *American Scientist* 98, No. 4 (2010), 311. https://doi.org/10.1511/2010.85.304.

141 S. Srinivasan and S. Ranganathan, *India's Legendary Wootz Steel: An Advanced Material of the Ancient World* (Hyderabad: University Press India Private Limited, 2014), 136.

142 Srinivasan and Ranganathan, *India's Legendary Wootz Steel: An Advanced Material of the Ancient World*, 133.

143 Srinivasan and Ranganathan, *India's Legendary Wootz Steel: An Advanced Material of the Ancient World*, 134.

144 R. B. Hargraves and R. W. Moir, "Liquid Fluoride Thorium Reactors," *American Scientist* 98, No. 4 (2010), 310-311. https://doi.org/10.1511/2010.85.304.

145 Hargraves and Moir, "Liquid Fluoride Thorium Reactors," *American Scientist* 98, No. 4, 306.

146 "Overview: The Thorium Molten Salt Reactor – Thorium MSR Foundation," n.d., https://www.thmsr.com/en/overview/#:~:text=Abundant%20energy&text=In%20case%20of%20an%20LWR,the%20same%20amount%20of%20energy.

147 R. B. Hargraves and R.W. Moir, "Liquid Fluoride Thorium Reactors," *American Scientist* 98, No. 4 (2010), 309. https://doi.org/10.1511/2010.85.304.

148 "Overview: The Thorium Molten Salt Reactor – Thorium MSR Foundation," n.d., https://www.thmsr.com/en/overview/#:~:text=Abundant%20energy&text=In%20case%20of%20an%20LWR,the%20same%20amount%20of%20energy.

149 R. B. Hargraves and R. W. Moir, "Liquid Fluoride Thorium Reactors," *American Scientist* 98, No. 4 (2010), 311. https://doi.org/10.1511/2010.85.304.

150 Hargraves and Moir, "Liquid Fluoride Thorium Reactors," *American Scientist* 98, No. 4, 313.

151 H. A. Shapiro, "Introduction," *The Cambridge Companion to Archaic Greece*, ed. H. A. Shapiro (Cambridge: Cambridge University Press, 2007), 1.

152 Jonathan M. Kenoyer, *Ancient Cities of the Indus Valley Civilization* (Karachi: Oxford University Press, 1998), 54.

153 D. P. Agrawal, *Harappan Technology and its Legacy* (New Delhi: Rupa and Company, 2009), 53.

154 Meera Nanda, "Hindutva's Science Envy," *Frontline*, September 16, 2016, 3.

https://web.archive.org/web/20170717173246/http://www.frontline.in/science-and-technology/hindutvas-science-envy/article9049883.ece.

Acknowledgments

THIS BOOK WOULD NOT EXIST WITHOUT A FEW BRAVE SOULS, generous minds, and some very persistent WhatsApp messages.

To Shikha Jain, who didn't just open doors, but also opened archives, field offices, and access to people who actually know history (hello, ASI). To Monika Bansal, who scoured the archives at the National Museum and caught historical errors before I made a fool of myself in print. And to Aradhana Pandey, the first editor, who ensured this manuscript didn't end up in the river Indrani by chapter three.

To my wife, Kanchan and my daughters, Neha and Naina, for being my constant support, letting me disappear into this story, and only occasionally pulling me out. To Vijay and Vivien for believing it was possible even when I wasn't so sure. And to Adit Bhargava, for being unclassifiable, unshakeable, and somehow always relevant. Grateful too for the support that poured in from extended family—it really does take a village, as I found out.

A big nod to Prabir Bhambal, publishing luminary and gentle encourager, who made the idea of finishing feel oddly possible.

To those who doubled as support infrastructure and comic relief: Nangla, Mukta, Kapil, Deepa, Raka, Hitesh—you endured my distracted dinners and missed calls with grace.

To Alok, Archana, Ashish, Chandni, Deepti, Harish, Harjeet, Hitesh, Jitender, Kamal, Ketaki, Milan, Mitesh, Namita, Neelu, Raj, Rishi, Roopak, Roopali, Sukesh, Varsha, Yashpal, and so many others—thanks for flooding my phone with more forwardable facts than most history classes. You knew what you were doing, and again, maybe not, but I appreciate it, and I salute you.

To the experts who generously shared knowledge deeper than Wikipedia's darkest corners: Dr. Abhick Sarkar, Dr. B. R. Mani, Prof. Jeevan Kharagwal, Prof. Jog Shree, Dr. Meera Das, Dr. Payel Sen, Dr. Pravin Misra, Dr. Rajesh Vatsa, Dr. Sharda Srinivasan, Prof. Dr. Vaishali—thank you for your patience, clarity, and for letting me ask just one more question. And thanks Department of Atomic Energy – experts in all things thorium.

To Anish and Anita Bhambal, your encouragement was just what the doctor ordered. And to Jaya Bhattacharya, Mita Kapur, Namita Gokhle, Paul Kumar, Shalini Shekhar, and many others who generously explained the intricacies of writing and the publishing world—thank you for your patience, insight, and for not rolling your eyes when I asked what a galley proof was.

To Kevin and his team—Navya, Sukanya, Tanvi, Archita, Kiran, and the talented folks behind the visuals and final push—thank you for having the faith to help this idea find its way into the world and onto a few bookshelves.

Finally, to Kabir and Reeya—thank you for living in my head, talking, arguing, dancing, and refusing to shut up until your story was told. I couldn't have done it without you. Literally.

Just wish Mom and Dad could have seen the finished form…